The Holdouts

The Holdouts

by

Sherry Clements

Drinian Press/
Huron, Ohio

This book is a work of fiction. As such, names, characters, incidents, and places (real or imagined) are used fictitiously and are products of the author's imagination. Any resemblance to persons, places, or actual events is coincidental.

Drinian Press
P.O. Box 63
Huron, Ohio 44839
Visit our Web site at: www.DrinianPress.com

Library of Congress Control Number: 2008939777

ISBN: 978-0-9820609-0-2

Printed in the United States of America

For my daughter,

Shawn Marie Hinson

Part I

Chapter One

Summer of Love, 1969

Mama dipped her toe out the door of the Greyhound bus like outside was a swimming pool, and she was testing the temperature. Spencer got off next, squalling and sucking his thumb. I hopped out, one, two, three; hot air rushed my skirt. A black bird caw-caw-cawing on a fence watched for a minute, but then flapped away. The afternoon had turned scorching, and the heat shimmered on the empty country highway. All the passengers gawked at us like we were putting on some kind of show for them. Mama turned her back to the windows, and Spencer begged to be picked up like he was three years old instead of six.

I checked my pocket to make sure my seashell was still there. It was the only thing I had time to grab when we were shoved out the front door, but I wouldn't have gone anywhere without it. No sir. Not even if they tortured me.

The bus driver dug out our big suitcase from the belly of the bus. "This is yours, ain't it?" He held up our suitcase. "It's the only one tied with twine."

Mama didn't answer or look up. With every mile on the bus, her bouffant hairdo had wilted. She kept poking bobby pins in it, but now it lay on her neck like a dead rat. Silent tears trickled down her face, smearing her makeup. I hadn't known what to do; I was no good with hair. So instead I stuck out my tongue at one old woman who kept peeking at us over the top of her book. I had a talent for this sort of thing and practiced all the time. People always said my face was going to freeze that way, and I sure hoped it would.

"I didn't have enough hair spray," Mama had confided, and I leaned close and nodded. It was the truth. She used the last of the Aqua Net that very morning and threw the can across the room. Right before she ordered me to go to the neighbor man's to borrow the telephone and call a cab to carry us to the bus station. *Franklin four oh three three three/the black and white cab company* jingled through my head.

The driver still held the suitcase. And while I was trying to figure out why he didn't just hand it to us, I couldn't help staring at his ears. They were big and wobbly, and they danced when he talked.

"Well, little lady," he continued yakking at Mama, "there'll be a bus going back later this evenin'."

"We won't be needing it," she mumbled.

"If you should change your mind..."

She took the suitcase from his hand, turned away. Never looked up. Spencer ran after her.

"Girl," said the bus driver.

That would be me. "Sir?"

"How old are you?"

"I'm ten."

He took a red bandana out of his back pocket and mopped his face.

Come to think of it, every old man I'd bothered to glance at had big ears. Most with hair sprouting out of them. I had brought up this subject once in a dinner conversation with the family. Daddy claimed that men born here in Arkansas grew ears big like that. He noted there was something in the air that made their ears keep ripening long after the rest of them had stopped. Then he wiggled his own to prove the point. Naturally, my daddy was a liar, so who could know the real reason?

The bus driver carefully folded his bandana and stuck it back in his pocket. "You take care of that mama of yours. She looks like she could use some help."

"Yes, sir." I looked around for my mama who needed some help, but she had already disappeared behind the bus with Spencer and the suitcase.

"White woman shouldn't be treated that way," he grumbled.

He wanted to say something else, but I needed to catch up, so I escaped the driver and his large ears and the bus and its cargo of bug-eyed people.

We stayed on the highway for a little while, then Mama turned down a dirt road, wobbling sideways in her high heels. The suitcase was heavy, and she kept switching it from hand to hand. Everyone who met my mama said she favored a glamorous young movie star, the dark-haired Natalie Wood. They wouldn't say that if they saw her right now.

Spencer took the thumb out of his mouth long enough to complain the rocks in the road were cutting his poor little feet to death, and his sneakers weren't helping him none. Mama didn't even look back. She kept walking fast, kicking up little dust clouds. Three bobby pins fell out of her hair, one after the other, and I was good and picked them up.

Was she sure this was the way to Grandma's house? Were we lost? Not even a taste of a breeze swept over us, and I was dying of thirst. I saw myself crawling on hands and knees, shriveled black tongue hanging out the side of my mouth: water...must have water....

There was no sense in asking any questions. She hadn't answered me in hours, telling me not to bother her. I was trying real hard not to bother her, but so much was happening. I was supposed to be quiet at a time like this, but I was excited. When we stepped on the Greyhound, I had put all my mixed up feelings in a wooden box and nailed it shut. Those rascals banged on the sides of the box, hollering to be let out.

A rock stood in my way, so I kicked it extra hard.

Barbwire fences rose on each side of us, and brown cows with white faces were chewing grass in the pastures. Real live cows. I admired the way they shimmied and shook the flies off, but they were indifferent as uppity cousins and snubbed us when we passed by. Did chocolate milk come from brown cows like them or was that just a story? I stopped in the middle of the road and closed my eyes to get a better picture. A pretty Elsie with long eyelashes popped into my head, an old woman with a three-legged stool and a shiny bucket, then me under a shade tree with a long tall glass and a chocolate moustache.

Spencer sneezed three times.

My lovely picture vanished. It had been dusty under the bed where me and him hid that morning. I shook my head clear of that thought and started walking again. I checked my pocket. Seashell still there. It felt cool to the touch, even on a day like today. Spencer would want to hear the waves if I took it out, so it stayed put. The shell was my most prized possession, and I had found it by accident one afternoon when I was rooting through the neighbor man's trash can. Imagine someone throwing away a shell. One day I would go to the ocean, and everything would be different there.

Something moving caught my eye.

There was this dust cloud coming down the road, coming toward us.

Out of the cloud stepped a rooster.

Still at a distance, but there was something in his strut that told me he was not a sweet fellow, like the grand-pappy roosters in Spencer's storybooks.

Now he was closer.

Feathers, every color of the rainbow, a red comb, bright and stiff, and a yellow beak at least three inches long, curled over his bottom lip like a fish hook. One eye on each side of his head, Egyptian style. Wicked claws just right for slicing human flesh.

I grabbed Spencer's hand and caught up with Mama.

"How much further?" I asked, knowing I had gone white around the gills.

She switched the suitcase and didn't answer. Patches of wet under her arms. The sun, low in the sky, still burning.

Now the rooster was a few feet away, watching us.

I hid behind her. Spencer hid behind me.

"Shoo," my mama said, like she was talking to a fly.

The rooster veered off our path, but not before he took my inventory. He blinked, and a dead film fell over his eye. *This ain't over, Sister.*

I walked backwards down the road. The rooster swiveled his head. When it was safe, I gave him the most horrible gesture I carried in my showcase of insults, the one involving an elbow, my left knee, and a mouthful of good spit. The rooster flung dirt at me.

But my mojo was bigger than his, and the battle was over. Stupid bird!

A few steps more and Mama stopped. She turned left and disappeared along a worn path that nobody saw but her. This time instead of snob cows on both sides, fat honeybees buzzing in clover gave way to friendly shade trees. A breeze stirred the air, so it wasn't quite as hot. We came to the end of the path and looked up to see a house. It was shabby with gray paint peeling, and the porch resting on stacks of bricks. A Henny Penny girl chicken scratched in the yard. Deep in the darkness of the porch, an old woman wearing overalls sat in a rocking chair.

Spencer took out his thumb and used it for a pointer: "There she is."

"I swore I'd never come back to this godforsaken place," muttered Mama.

The old woman snapped beans from a pan like the women who sat on porches at home. She glanced up.

"Lookee here, lookee here," she sang out, "look what the cat drug in."

The old woman put down the pan and stepped off the porch, man-sized rubber boots floppy on her feet, her brown face crinkled with pleasure. About halfway across the yard, when she could see us clearly, she came to a dead halt. She looked at Mama's broken nose, then at Spencer and me, then back at Mama.

Mama didn't say anything, just stood there holding the heavy suitcase with both hands. Every line on her face turned down.

Then the old woman walked straight over and picked up Spencer. He laid his head on her shoulder like he had always known her.

"Hi, Grandma," I said. "I'm Martha."

She put her arm around me and took us all into her home.

"The milk is always white, no matter the color of the cow," Grandma explained, when I asked what the deal was with that.

The next morning in the barn, I put out the feed while she milked. The sound of the siss siss siss hitting the side of the bucket brought the mouser cat running. She me-yowled until Grandma gave her a squirt. We carried some into the house and sold the extra down the road to the neighbor who wasn't lucky enough to have her own milk department.

"A fine helper you got there," the lady of the house said.

From the first day, I never missed an early morning in the barn.

Spencer and me picked so many blackberries our fingers turned purple. Grandma made pies with the bounty, and I loved watching her brown hands in white flour. Sometimes she'd watch me watching her, and she'd touch my nose with flour and smile. Like I'd been crowned Queen of England, I'd walk straight all day.

Late every afternoon when it was Death Valley hot, and we felt too lazy to do anything else, we packed a gallon jar of ice tea (three inches of sugar in the bottom of the jug) and marched single-file through the tall grass to the pond. Grandma always went first with her cane pole and tackle box. I carried Spencer piggyback part of the way, even though he was almost as big as me. He all ready had so many chigger bites from playing in the pastures he was one big itch. Dragonflies hovered in the hazy air around our heads. Spencer believed me when I told him that fairy princes rode their backs, and he always looked for a coat of arms and a little tiny lance. Once we came upon a dead turtle. The smell stupefied.

"Looks like dinner," I teased, making him howl.

Sometimes Mama went with us, always bringing up the caboose. She sat under a shade tree and read our horoscopes from old movie magazines. Every now and then she smiled a little and forgot to touch her nose.

"Martha," she said, "you will discover great riches in your future. Spencer, beware of the number three, and, Mother, a tall handsome stranger will drop by unexpectedly so be prepared.

"I will," Grandma answered. "I'll lock my doors."

She showed us how to bait our hooks with a wiggle worm. The first fish I caught was small, just a flash of silver.

"Put him back," Grandma said. "He ain't finished."

"A little taste is better than nothing," Mama answered. "Keep him."

But when she wasn't looking, I slipped him off the stringer and let him swim away. Spencer saw, but for once he didn't snitch.

Here, I could have seven adventures before seven in the morning, and they kept coming till bedtime. At home when Daddy walked through the door late in the day, we had to stop what we were playing and sniff the air to see what kind of mood he was in. Would it be jokes and stories? Or would Spencer and me need a place to hide out before the night was over? So what would happen this time? Would Mama and Daddy make up like always? Mama hadn't liked it here when she was growing up, what with no one to dress up for and her most intimate friends being cows and all. Once when she was sitting on the back step alone, lighting one cigarette from the butt of the next, I tried asking her.

"What's going to happen to us?" I said.

She stared like I was a rude stranger, then turned her face away into the cloud of smoke. She didn't talk if she didn't feel like it, especially to me.

That evening at home, we fried the fish for supper. When we had finished picking through the bones, Grandma grabbed her straw hat off the hook by the door and plopped it on her head.

"Time to hoe the tomatoes," she said. "I'll see y'all later."

Grandma gardened by the moon signs in the Farmer's Almanac.

"That hat looks like something a mule would wear," Mama called out.

"Heee-hawww," Grandma answered as she disappeared out back.

Spence and me cracked up.

I tried snorting milk out my nose and got choked instead. Mama didn't pay any attention, just kept picking at her food. At home, a milk snorting show would have earned me at least a slap from her. She despised my tomboy ways. She would say "boys will be boys" anytime Spencer did something crass and exciting. But if I showed off, she didn't have a ready-made explanation for it. Often, I left her speechless. I puffed up my chest.

Then before we could clear the table, someone knocked on the front door.

"Is it Daddy?" Spencer asked.

"It's not!" I kicked him under the table. You'd know Daddy's loud car from miles away. If he pulled up in your front yard, there wouldn't be any question.

"Go see, kids." Mama hopped up from the table. "I want to check my hair."

Spencer popped in his thumb, and we went to the living room. Had the rooster figured out how to knock on the door? Instead three old women stood on the porch. One had a bowling ball of hair. One's bosom touched her belly. One held a tambourine. All three carried Holy Bibles and white handkerchiefs. Purses as big as suitcases dangled from their elbows.

"Is your grandmother here?" said Big Bosom.

"She's out back in the garden," I said. "I'll go get her."

Big Bosom fluttered her hands in the air like little bird wings. "Oh, no, no, no, that won't be necessary."

The ladies smiled slyly and looked pleased.

"We're from the Holy Ghost Temple," Bowling Ball began.

"You must be Pixie's children," said Big Bosom. "Y'all have her big brown eyes."

Tambourine Woman shook her agreement.

"Yes, ma'am." The three of us did have brown eyes, except Spencer had long dark eyelashes, too, and scrutiny of them always caused Mama to sigh and say, "*no fair.*"

Bowling Ball leaned toward Spencer. "You a mighty big boy to be sucking your thumb that way."

Big Bosom said, "Don't you know that will buck your teeth?"

Tambourine woman jangled a warning.

Immediately, Spencer popped the thumb out of his mouth and stared cross-eyed at it. He hid the thumb in his pocket.

Church people were always knocking on the door back home and asking me if I was ready to meet my maker. "Are you saved, little girl?" I didn't know how to answer.

"Your mama was a member of our flock when she was a child. Bet she told you all about us," said Bowling Ball.

"No, ma'm," I answered. "Not once."

"Honey, go get Pixie," said Big Bosom. "Now."

Tambourine woman shook *hurry up*.

Big Bosom was in charge of this posse, and I was not the outlaw she had come for.

Mama walked into the living room and said *come in, come in* to the ladies. She had powdered her nose. They sat down, and she sent me for ice tea. It took awhile to figure out where Grandma kept the company glasses. By the time I got back, they were all down on their knees praying with their arms snaking around Mama and Spencer. I set the tea down on the coffee table and turned to sneak back out. But Mama grabbed and pulled me down beside her.

"Jesus, bring your little lost lambs back into the flock," they all wailed.

Soon Mama was crying, Spencer was crying, and I was, too. That hard floor really hurt my bony knees. They didn't stop until I pretended to faint. Spencer fell over, too, and spoiled my act. He was so ignorant. Mama moved to get a switch, but Big Bosom called out. Her knees had locked in place, and Mama helped her up instead.

"Anything for the Lord," Bosom said after she caught her breath.

Later Grandma came in carrying bright red tomatoes in her old mule hat. We sat at the kitchen table while Mama stood at the sink and washed dishes. Grandma sliced her tomatoes.

"Some church ladies were here," I said.

She stopped slicing in midair and turned toward Mama.

"Who was it, Pixie?"

Mama answered without turning around. "You know."

Grandma put the knife beside the plate.

"One had hair like this," Spencer raised his arms above his head in a circle.

"One was out to here." I imitated Big Bosom's big bosoms.

"And the other one?" Grandma shook an imaginary tambourine, and its rattle filled the kitchen.

We laughed. Mama didn't.

"They don't like me," said Grandma.

Spencer and me looked at each other. Who could not like Grandma?

"They say I'm a sinner 'cause I don't like to sit in a box every Sunday."

Mama sniffed.

Grandma ignored.

Spencer asked, "What kind of box?"

"She means church." I explained to the small dumb boy.

"You called them heifers." Mama added.

Grandma admitted: "That I did."

A feeling of deliciousness started at my dirty toes and climbed all the way up my body. My eyes brightened. My mouth watered. I had a wicked grandma.

"I didn't like what they was teaching your mama. All them rules."

Mama turned from the sink. "Jesus is love is what they was teaching."

Grandma started to say something else, but Mama walked out of the room.

We left the tomatoes unsliced and moved into the living room. Grandma rocked in the rocking chair and told us about her God: the God who loved all people, the God who would take up the very worst among us and hold that one the closest.

"Does he have a beard?" Spencer wanted to know.

We acted out the whole evening show for her. Spencer stuffed a pillow in his shirt and pretended to be Bosom stuck in the praying position. I pulled him up from behind while his arms windmilled, karate chopping his bony knees so he could stand up straight. Grandma laughed until she got a stitch in her side. She kept saying, *do that part again.* After three standing ovations, Spencer and me ran out the door and cartwheeled off the porch. We danced a dance without music in the dew grass while up above us, the wishing stars raced across the night sky.

One Tuesday, shortly after the cock-a-doodle-do went off, we were gathered in the kitchen to fix breakfast. It was our biggest meal since Grandma liked to cook early before it got too hot.

"Martha," she asked, "do you want to set the table?"

"I can't," I said, "I'm gonna sit on the chester drawers and kill flies."

"Well, that's important, too." She went back to frying bacon at the stove.

The chest of drawers was an old brown one that stood in the corner. Tucking the swatter in the back pocket of my shorts, I pulled each drawer open a little and used those like a ladder. I had to be careful, though, because one of my knees had thirteen scabs on it, thirteen bad luck scabs.

I settled on top, pushing all the junk to the side. I liked it up here; I could see everything. Mama sat at the table sipping black coffee from a cracked cup. Grandma tried to fatten up Spencer, who was so skinny he looked like he had no mother. After the bacon fried, Grandma wiped the iron skillet clean with a slice of light bread.

"Yum-yum," she said, handing the greasy bread to him.

He played on the linoleum with a toy truck. When Grandma turned her back, he pinched off a little piece of the crust and rolled it between his hands. Soon the truck had enough balls of dough to carry to the dump.

"He's wasting that bread." I pointed my swatter at him. They ignored my attempt to get Spencer to straighten up and fly right.

He gave a little secret smile knowing he had gotten away with his usual criminal behavior.

I thought about climbing down and swatting him, but it was too much trouble. Instead, I examined my bad knee. There was always a few scabs on my knees, but I thought this might be a new world's record and should be reported to the authorities. I might get wrote up in a medical journal.

"Would y'all look at this?" I said, "I have thirteen scabs on one knee."

Mama carefully sat down her coffee cup. "Your daddy always says that I have the smallest knees he ever saw, on a grown human being, that is."

I opened my mouth to answer.

Mama smiled at me, patiently waiting for my reply.

This time I couldn't think of anything to say.

But Grandma could.

"Since you brought him up," she said, standing at the stove with her back to us, "what happened, Pixie?"

Mama picked up the good knife and started peeling an onion for the fried potatoes. "What do you mean, Mother?"

"What happened to your nose?"

A hush fell over the room. A hush fell over my heart.

"Oh, you know me," Mama finally answered. "Clumsy."

Spencer's face said that he had turned on the key in his worry ignition and the engine started fine. He drove his toy truck over to Mama's chair.

A green fly buzzed at the screen door. It couldn't find the hole where it had come in, frantically searching from corner to corner.

"Don't flip out," I whispered to the fly.

"Buzz, buzz," he cried.

Mama cut her eyes at Spencer and me, then looked back at Grandma. It meant, don't talk in front of the kids.

Grandma heard the fly. She opened the back door and set it free. Turning back, she glanced at me. "Be careful up there, Missy. I don't want you to fall off."

Something in her face told me I could go ahead and say it.

"Grandma."

She waited.

I took a deep breath then blurted it out.

"Daddy hit her."

"Now why do you want to talk like that for? You know it was an accident." Mama chopped the onion and the knife went whack whack whack. "You think you know something about being married?"

I stared at my scabs and hoped to God that I never would since all married people did was sit around the kitchen table while the husband talked about the work he couldn't find, and the wife talked about the bills they couldn't pay. It was miserable.

"Martha," Grandma said, "why don't you go outside and gather some eggs for our breakfast? And Spencer, would you go make your bed?"

"Yes ma'm." Leaving was a good idea. I needed to get out of there before Mama decided I was the one who had busted her nose. I climbed down and went to the back door. Spencer raced his truck toward the bedroom with his skinny behind sticking up in the air.

"Where's the rooster?" I always checked before stepping out of the house alone, never forgetting the hate in his eye that first day.

"He was in front last time I looked," Grandma said, "shaking his tail feathers for whoever might be watching."

I picked up the egg basket and went outside, hanging around the back door for a minute until Mama said, "*go Martha.*" The henhouse stood at the edge of the yard right where the cow pasture started. I walked slowly down the path, but they didn't talk again until I was halfway there, and I couldn't make out the words.

The latch on the henhouse door lifted easily, and the door swung open. I checked for egg-sucking weasels before I stepped in, peering into all the dark corners. Grandma had all kinds of weird stories about egg-sucking weasels including one about a cad who was so bold, he'd come knocking on the henhouse door, and when a chicken answered, he was standing there with a suitcase, smiling like a Bible salesman.

Sunlight fell through cracks in the ceiling and made ribbons of light in the air. Red-feathered chickens snuggled in their nests of straw. They softly cackled hello like ladies at a tea party. The smells of straw and dust and little warm bodies blended together and made me ah-choo.

"Bless you," I heard one say from the corner of my mind.

I walked over to the first lovely.

"Henny Penny, what are you sittin' on?" I slipped my hand under her just like Grandma showed me. Gently, gently. My fingers touched a warm egg, and it went in the basket. She fussed a little and showed me her feathers.

"There'll be more where that one came from," I reassured her. Grandma said you had to speak sweetly. One by one my basket filled up with brown eggs. In spite of time spent at tea parties, they were all hardworking birds. Mama sent me to the corner grocery many a time to buy a half-dozen eggs. I had never known what I was missing: soft feathers, the smell of clean straw, small talk.

"So long, ladies. See you tomorrow."

They murmured: "Good-bye, Martha, dear. Sweet child."

I looked back fully expecting them to be waving dainty lace handkerchiefs in the air. Did one touch a wing to her beak and blow me a kiss? No. They were not Hollywood chickens.

Then I stepped out of the henhouse, and he was waiting on the path.

Just the sight of him was an attack, and my heart flip-flopped. Was he angry? I couldn't tell. He looked the same. His feathers were shiny and unruffled, his beak, still three inches long and curved like a fishhook. The same as when I made the insulting gesture in the road with the spit, the elbow, and the left knee.

Sure wished I hadn't done that.

"Am I in your way, Mister?" I stepped to the right, giving him plenty of room to pass by.

He stepped to the right.

He was a smart rooster. Had he escaped from an old-timey traveling show? The rooster swiveled his head and pecked at something on his back. He probably had fleas which would explain his contrary mood.

The dead eyes blinked once, twice.

"Grandma...." I called out in a feeble little voice. Mama had sharp ears, and Grandma, a double mother, had sharper.

The rooster raised his head and looked right at me. His dead eyes sent a message: *they can't hear you.*

I took a step to the left.

He took a step to the left.

It only made them madder when you acted scared because if you were about to get it, it was only, by God, because you had asked for it. So I gripped the egg basket and put the other hand in my pocket and jiggled my change and whistled a little tune between my teeth and looked at the bright blue sky as if I were checking on the weather.

The rooster turned in a circle three times, then settled in the dirt.

This could be a trick.

I stepped back to the right and slowly edged around him, still whistling, still jiggling. The smell of my sweat flooded my nose, and it was the nervous sweat of a grown-up woman.

He swiveled his head and picked his fleas, all casual now.

My nonchalant attitude may have fooled him. He understood that I would not go down without a squawk. Cautiously, I inched forward.

Another step, now I was around him, and he was still acting like a normal bird. One step past, and there was nothing between me and the back door. Wait until I told them about this. They'd be sorry they ran me out of the house. Sorry they sent me out here with a misfit rooster on the loose. They were going to hear about this, all right.

Then the wind came, and the wind was the warning.

He swooped on me, almost knocking me down, but he couldn't hold on.

"Grandma," I cried. "Mama."

He spread his wings. He scratched the dirt. His beak darted in and out, ripping the air. He crowed.

I own you, sister. You're all mine.

I didn't run. I stood there with my shoulders hunched and stared at the ground. The rooster circled. I watched him without moving. Then I could feel him behind me, and the hair stood up on my neck. He was silent, circling.

Sound carried from the house. The murmur of Grandma's voice rose, then fell. The oven door opened and closed.

I was paralyzed.

In the house, a chair scraped across the floor.

He slammed into me again, and this time it was the way he wanted it. His beak sliced me, each cut on fire.

The pain screamed *move it, girl!* and that broke the spell. I ran towards the house, as fast as I could run. My basket flew into the air, and the eggs rained down.

Wings flapping, he sliced and diced me with daggers.

I tripped and fell in the tall grass.

"Grandma!"

He flapped his wings and dug in tighter. He flapped his wings so hard he blocked out the sun. He flapped his wings faster and faster and faster, and I knew he was going to pick me up and fly away forever. I grabbed the grass, held on, and screamed bloody murder.

Grandma ran out the back door and snatched the rooster off me. I reached back. My fingers came away bright red. She flicked her wrist and snapped the rooster's neck. Before the screen door slammed shut, that bird was dead. His spirit flew out of him like a tornado of angry stinging bees.

She dropped the rooster on the ground, gathered me up.

I cried and cried and cried.

I didn't know if I could ever stop.

We rocked in the dirt of the yard for a long time.

"He'll never hurt you again," she said over and over.

Mama and Spencer came out of the house and respectfully stood by.

Finally, when my neck stopped glowing with pain, I bent down to look at the beast. I glanced up at Grandma just for a little reassurance. She nodded. I took a big breath and poked him with my big toe. He was dead all right. She patted me one more time like she was really proud of me.

I blew my nose three or four times on my shirt tail. Mama went for the ointment for my rooster bites. She brought a warm rag and wiped off the blood on my neck, dabbed on the medicine.

"You have egg on your head," Spencer pointed out. Then he walked up to the dead rooster and nudged it with his toe.

"Squawk!" I yelled and threw out my hand.

Spencer jumped twelve feet back.

"She's going to be o.k." Grandma got up from the ground, went digging around in the barn, and walked back carrying an old black pot. Mama gathered wood. I struck the match. Soon fire roared under the pot. The lady chickens came out of their henhouse and sniffed at the rooster. They cackled and scratched victory in the dirt. Grandma poured boiling water over the old dead thing. Spencer and me plucked the many-colored feathers, and they flew into the air and made a rainbow in the sunshine.

We inspected the rooster, now just a naked bird.

"Not much meat at all," Grandma said, "there never is on a rooster."

Then in the fresh air even the smell of his hot pickled flesh disappeared.

She sure was lucky to have my help.

"We really killed him, didn't we, Grandma?"

Spencer interrupted. "But you didn't kill–"

Mama swiveled her head and gave Spencer the stink eye. The words dried up and fell off his tongue.

The tail feathers went into my hair, and I danced a warpath around the yard. Spencer could barely keep up with me, pitiful, pitiful. I grabbed Grandma's sharp knife for my tomahawk and scared two frogs and a grasshopper, afraid of losing their hair. Then the mouser cat came sniffing around, and I threatened to give her whiskers a trim. She trembled on sock feet. Mama took the knife away from me, but she let me carry an old ball-peen hammer. My arm shook as I raised it to the sky.

"I am Mighty Martha, the great chicken killer!"

The sun threw a cloud arm over his eyes to block the terrible sight of me.

It was way past breakfast by then and getting close to the time Grandma called dinner. Mama put the skillet on, loaded it with lard, and fried the bird a golden brown. Spencer and I got a leg and thigh each. We still had the bacon and potatoes from the forgotten breakfast. I put the hammer down beside my plate. Spencer tried to sneak it.

I waved a leg bone at him. "This leg was walking around a few minutes ago. Look at it now."

He drew his hand back.

Mama nibbled on a breast, and Grandma ate the rest. We sat back full and shiny with grease. It was a mighty fine meal. I belched my appreciation, just like they do in China. Grandma pulled a little silver can from her overalls and loaded her bottom lip with snuff. Mama talked about a special egg rinse for body-and-shine and said I was going to have the prettiest hair around. Then she picked through the mess on the table and came up with the wishbone for Spencer and me. We pulled on it, and I got the short piece. I wished we could live with Grandma forever.

Each night we slept on our mama's old feather mattress on the floor. Bouncing up and down, we sang *five little monkeys jumping on the bed/one fell off and hurt her head.* Grandma came in and clicked her teeth at us, so we stopped. Spencer took all the frogs out of his pockets and handed them to me. I kissed them one by one, then we waited to see if they had been under a spell.

"Kissing frogs is a good way to get dirt in your teeth, Martha." Grandma snapped a sheet over the bed with Spencer and me in it, and the sheet floated down, soft on our bodies, tickling our skin.

After Spencer started snoring, Mama came in and sat beside me.

"I have something to show you." She handed me a photograph. It was them when they were young, standing arm in arm. Daddy looked straight at the camera grinning, but Mama was looking up at Daddy. I tried to see what she saw. He had on jeans, rolled up at the cuff, a white t-shirt. His dark hair was slicked back, like how he still wore it. Was he mean way back then? He liked to tell stories about high school fights, but they were always with armed bullies twice his size.

"Wasn't he handsome?" she said. "Everyone says he looks Italian."

"I guess."

Mama was the pretty one. The picture was in black and white, but I recognized her red sundress with the spaghetti straps and her big gold hoop earrings. With all that and her hair in a French twist, she really did look like a movie star.

"He was the new boy in school, and all the girls were dying to go out with him," she said. "He could have had anyone." She patted her hair. "But he wanted me."

I took a good look at her. She had on lipstick, her hair fixed even now at bedtime. Then I understood. She had been waiting on him this whole time.

"I was the chosen one." Mama used a voice I didn't know. "I felt so special." She stared at the photograph. "We had dreams, too, me and your daddy. Our lives were going to be different. Easier. That's why we left here." She sat on the bed a while longer without saying anything else. When every corner of the room was completely filled up with her sadness, she turned off the lamp and drifted away in the darkness.

I laid there as long as I could stand it, then reached under the mattress where I'd hidden my treasure seashell the first night we were here. I groped, then my hand closed around it. The shell whispered in my ear while I watched shadows dance on the wall. She told me not to cry. She told me stories about the ocean, and all the good things that happened there. She told me about warm sand and the sound seagulls made and how no two waves were ever the same.

Pretty soon I could see it.

The perfect hiding place was behind the divan in the living room, but Spencer found me anyway.

"Bang! Bang!" He blew smoke from the barrel of his six-shooter. "I got you, Martha. Come out of there right now and act dead."

I crawled from behind the divan. He had missed, so I planned to make a run for it.

Spencer stared out the window. Then *he* ran out the door. Daddy stood in the front yard. He snatched up Spencer in a bear hug. I drew my gun from its holster, carefully aimed, and shot Spencer in the back of the head.

Mama went outside and talked to Daddy. They made Spencer come back in the house. I couldn't catch my breath. Grandma had to take a BC Powder, the strongest aspirin ever invented, the kind a lady would pack in her purse before she left the house for her father's funeral. Grandma opened the little slip of wax paper that held the powder, tilted her head back, let the grains slide under her tongue. Then she and I sat on the divan and held hands. Every line in her face turned down.

I couldn't tell Grandma how I felt because I knew I would start blubbering. They'd get mad at me. We weren't allowed to cry unless we had hurt ourselves, and there was a three minute time limit on that. All the old laws were back in place.

Mama came in a few minutes later and pulled the suitcase out from under the bed. It was already packed. She walked around the house and gathered up the last of our things.

"Thank you, Mother." She kissed my grandma on the cheek.

"Come back anytime, Pixie, my sweet." Grandma lifted her hand to touch Mama's hair, but Mama was already gone.

Daddy honked the horn.

I didn't want anything ugly to happen in front of Grandma, so I squared my shoulders and walked across the porch and got in my place beside Spencer in the backseat. The sweet smell of Daddy's Vitalis hair oil and Juicy Fruit chewing gum filled the air.

Grandma stood at the car. "Wouldn't you like to come in and have a cool drink?" she asked him.

"No, ma'am, places to go, people to see." He popped his gum and threw his arm over the seat and looked at me. "I got me a good job this time, Martha, driving a truck and delivering bread for the big bakery. We can get you that Chatty Cathy you been wanting."

I hadn't played with dolls in about a hundred years.

"Oh goody," I said.

They stared. Mama's face said: don't you dare mess this up. Daddy's face said: have you forgotten who I am?

Grandma leaned into the backseat and kissed us.

Spencer told her, "I'll come for you when I am old enough to marry."

She answered, "I'll be waiting. I will make us a pie."

I slipped the seashell out of my pocket and handed it to her through the open window. She tucked it in her pocket without asking any questions, then her strong fingers held mine.

Daddy reached under the dashboard and put two wires together. It didn't catch until the second time. He pushed the gas pedal, and I had to let go. Spencer and me waved out the back window until Grandma and the little farm disappeared, and I kept waving a long time after that.

Chapter Two

What They're Wearing in Paris, 1969

Diane Bickerstaff Buck was the Queen of the fifth grade, always surrounded by the top girls, ladies-in-waiting. They were everything I wasn't: small boned and blonde with a tricky way of talking. They lived in brick houses. One day Diane came to school with a mole drawn on her cheek like Ginger on Gilligan's Island, and the next day every girl in class had one, except for me and the Holy Roller. I would have had one except Mama caught me going out the door and made me wash it off.

There were some others who would never be top girls: the five Holy Rollers. All sisters, last name Spoon. Round faced and pudgy from the oldest to the youngest. We didn't have many of their kind since most of them went to Buckeye Christian School over by the railroad tracks. You had to pay to go there, and I guessed their parents couldn't afford to send five girls. The Spoons were tormented because of their funny Holy Roller outfits. They had long stringy hair and dresses that almost touched their ankles when all the other girls were going pixie. It was legal to wear your hem three inches above the knee, and in the history of the school, no teacher had ever pulled out the measuring tape for a Spoon. It wasn't just their clothes. They didn't join in things like normal kids.

"It's a sin," one would squeak when asked why. The way they walked the halls with their heads hanging down made them easy targets. Even the teachers talked behind their hands.

Only the middle Spoon was different. I had her in my class, and every time a blondie squealed about the latest fashion this girl raised one bushy black eyebrow as if she were top dog, and they were the fleas. She was usually the last one picked for the team since choices were based on popularity. I tried not to sniffle when it happened to me, but the middle Spoon strolled out to right field, laid down in the dandelions, and took a nap. Somebody had to go wake her up when the game was over. That girl reminded me of my grandma who didn't give a hoot about what people thought either. I wanted to buy the middle Spoon a carton of chocolate milk that she didn't have to share with anyone else. I wanted to defend her when the kids played cootie tag and tried to make her "it." I wanted to braid her straggle hair smooth, tie a red ribbon on the end, and watch the eyebrow shoot up at the mention of doing something so girly. I worked on my approach, but in class she gave the evil eye to anyone who came close. Outside and in the cafeteria, she hung out with her dumb sisters.

One cold December day, when pictures of snowmen and striped candy canes lined the walls, the bell rang for recess. The principal, an old woman, but not as old as my grandma, directed traffic in the hall. The little kids believed that she kept a black tabby and a broomstick. She wore cat's eye glasses with diamonds twinkling in the corners of the frames. The glasses magnified her eyes and made them look larger than a regular person's. Heavy, gold earbobs hung from her ears like snapping turtles. Every morning the principal put her hair up in a smart bun and stabbed it with a pencil.

I leaned on the wall and slid down the hall, and her eyes shined like a spotlight. I checked to make sure eve-rything was zipped, buttoned, tucked in, and tied. My sneakers had holes; I curled my toes so they wouldn't poke out. My mama's worn out old coat flapped around my knees. Once the coat had real pearl buttons, but they had fallen off and lost themselves long ago. She replaced them one by one with whatever was at the bottom of her sewing box. Now there was a big brass button hanging by one thread, a wooden button in the shape of an anchor, and three plaid. At home when I complained, suddenly my story would change and be about Daddy. What *he* had to wear to school, what people said, and how he held his head high. Good for him, but I hated it.

Keeping my head down and my nose clean, I rounded the corner. I would not go to recess. I had a better idea about how to spend my time. Today I would make an unauthorized visit to the library. When we came to the library door, I bent down and faked tying my shoe. All the top girls strolled by, giggling. Then the rest of the class, including my teacher, moved past like water flowing around a stone in the middle of a stream. I stood up, made a quick left, and walked into the library just like I was supposed to be there.

It was empty of people, except the sixth grade girl stamping books at the checkout desk. Winter sunlight slanted in through tall windows. Dust hovered in the air. A bird flew by outside, but it was only a shadow in the distance. The screams of kids playing at recess faded away. I breathed the stillness. Slowly I walked down the stacks of books, running my finger along the spine of each one.

I did not read books about girls who kept a lipstick in their pockets. I did not read books about girls who rescued wild animals and studied to be nurses. I did not read books about girls who were waiting for a prince. I read books about girls who went adventuring. There were two or three of them. Mostly, I read books about boys.

Then I tripped over a kid crouching down in the stacks. Righting myself, I realized it was Shelby from my class. He had red hair and freckles. All the kids said *better dead than red on the head.* I liked him anyway. He lived on my street.

Shelby looked up. "How much trouble am I in?"

"You're not in trouble," I answered. "Not yet anyway."

"They didn't send you here to get me?" he asked.

"No."

Shelby looked puzzled.

"Then what are you doing here?"

"Came to read books."

We grinned.

Shelby patted the floor beside him. "Sit down, old girl."

I sat cross legged beside him, and my clothes didn't matter.

He had been to the ocean. His grandparents had taken him to Galveston, Texas when he was little, and he remembered most of it: drinking fresh coconut milk straight from the hairy brown shell, watching lovely hula girls tell stories with their hands, and once on the horizon, a ship flying the skull and crossbones. Someday I would live on the beach and never need shoes again.

I begged, "Tell me some more about the ocean."

"I can do better than that."

He crawled on his belly across the floor, stuck his head out at the end of the stack and checked both ways. Satisfied no enemy was in sight, he crawled across the aisle, grabbed a book, and crawled back.

It was an atlas. He flipped over to Texas and pointed at Galveston.

"This is it," he said. "That's where I've been."

I examined the atlas closely.

We estimated it would take three days to get there by fast car. Shelby pulled a piece of paper from his notebook and wrote the directions for me. We were so busy we didn't hear footsteps.

The librarian tapped me on the shoulder. "The principal wants to see you in her office."

Shelby and I jumped to our feet.

"Not you," she said to him. "Martha only."

"What do you want me to do?" he asked.

"Keep reading."

I quickly folded the directions and stuck them in my shoe in case jail time was involved.

Shelby bowed his head as if he were already at my funeral.

I pulled the old coat tight around me and walked out of the library.

In the principal's waiting room, the smallest Spoon sat. She had wet her pants again. She slumped in the chair with her chin on her chest, her feet barely touching the floor, not making a sound, with tears rolling down her little pie face. I looked through my pockets for a stick of Juicy Fruit because sometimes that's all it took to cheer up a second grader. My hands came up empty. I didn't know what to do with them, so I sent them on another errand, this time scratching old chigger bites down around my ankles. I hadn't expected to be sent here. Usually just rough boys were called in to the principal's office, rough boys who hawked snot right on the ground and ran around snapping the back of any girl's bra, any girl who was fool enough to wear one. Not me. I was all Tom Sawyer and no Becky. The boys left me alone. All Tom Sawyer and no Huck Finn, too, and navigating through the day was like being on a small raft rushing down the wide Mississippi.

Then the principal finally opened the door to her office and stepped into the room. I jumped up and stood at attention. I thought about saluting.

"Good afternoon, Martha." She ignored the littlest Spoon.

"Afternoon, ma'am." That woman had a lot of teeth, and she was showing me every one. Were they real?

"This is your lucky day," she said.

I gave her a crippled little smile, not so sure that I believed her.

"I noticed that you need a coat."

So this wasn't about the unauthorized visit to the library.

"No ma'am, I already have a coat." I stretched my arms wide as if to say, *and see here it is.* The brass button chose that moment to let go. It dropped to the floor, so heavy that it spun around where it landed, clanging like a hubcap that had fallen off a car.

We all stared at it, the littlest Spoon, the principal, and me. I counted seventeen of my own heartbeats.

The principal cleared her throat.

"Let's go look in the clothes closet and see if we can find you a better one." She pushed me toward the door. Over her shoulder, she barked instructions to the secretary about the little Spoon. "Get one of her sisters to come clean her up."

I followed her down the hall to the tiny room they called the clothes closet. My parents weren't going to like this. Mama and Daddy owned they were humble people and proud of it. They taught Spencer and me to always choose the least of things. Daddy preached when you take handouts from people, you had to take whatever else they wanted to hand out with it. The principal flipped on the light and started going through racks of clothes. I stood at the door with my arms folded and didn't go in.

Then she pulled *it* off the rack.

"What about this one?" She held the coat up for me to see. It was black and shiny, probably made from a wild mountain panther. The collar was leopard spot. It was the most perfect thing I'd ever seen, and it drew me into the room.

"Try it on," she said.

The panther wasn't too big or too little. It was just right. "I don't think my mama and daddy will let me have it." I stroked the panther fur.

"There's a mirror on the door," she said.

I looked like I had come straight from Paris, France. I should be walking a poodle, wearing a slanted hat, carrying a little purse with a silver buckle. I was a Paris regular in this coat and well acquainted with both cathedrals and catacombs. It no longer mattered that my skirt was patched, my ankles were dirty, and my sneakers had holes in them.

The principal picked up my old coat and tossed it into a cardboard box in the corner. "Martha, we don't like our students looking like little beggars. Now you take that coat home. Tell them I said."

My mama had sat on the couch under the lamp sewing on the old coat, concentrating with all her might, trying to make it right. She spent a whole lot of time in la-la land these days; it was hard to get her attention. But she had taken the time to try to make the coat decent.

The principal woman sped out of the room. I ran after her.

"Ma'am," I said, "wait."

She paused with her hand on the doorknob to the office and turned her headlights on me. Her glasses glittered, and the snapping turtles hung on for dear life.

I started slipping the coat off. "Mama and Daddy—"

"But you look so special, Martha."

Hesitating, I searched her face.

Slowly she reached over and straightened my collar. "You could be a lovely girl."

Me? A lovely girl? Had she just said that?

The coat put itself back on. The buttons buttoned. The pockets called my fingers home.

"It's yours," the principal whispered.

Then she showed me her teeth again, all forty-seven, and disappeared through her office doorway.

What could I do?

The bell rang for recess.

I walked out into the perfect winter day wearing the panther coat with the leopard spot collar. The sun shone in the schoolyard. Kids ran, jumped, skipped, and screamed all around me. Shelby ran up carrying a book under his arm, but since I had become a Paris regular, I gave him a wave and kept going. Special, lovely me strolled over to the monkey bars. All the top girls were gathered there like the birds in that Hitchcock movie. It was cold enough for breath to show, and they puffed on pretend cigarettes. They leaned over and checked me out. I set my face on the smile channel and waited. Finally, Diane Bickerstaff Buck spoke.

"Come on up," she said. It was the first time she had been nice to me since the first grade when I told her there was no such thing as Santa Claus. I climbed up, one cold bar at a time, and sat on the end.

"I want to sit by Martha."

The girls let the Queen pass until she was next to me.

"Nice coat," she said and stroked the fur.

"Really nice," said all her ladies-in-waiting.

"Thank you," I purred.

"Where'd you get it?" she asked.

"My grandma sent it to me."

"Where'd she get it?"

"Africa. She bagged a panther on safari and made it into a coat for me."

The Queen rolled her eyes, and all the ladies giggled.

"No, really, where'd you get it?" she asked again.

"Woolworth's. Downtown."

"I'll have to get my mother to take me," said the Queen.

"Me too. Me too," agreed all the ladies.

"Was it in the Junior Department or in Girl's?" asked the Queen.

Something caught my eye a few feet away.

"What's going on over there?" Everyone looked where I'd pointed.

A crowd gathered quickly.

"It's a fight," yelled a boy high on the swings. He hit the ground running.

"Who's fighting?" asked the Queen, but we couldn't see.

"Probably just a couple of sixth graders." I wanted their attention back on me. "Well, does anyone know what we're having for lunch?"

Nobody answered. They kept craning their necks to see.

Then the crowd parted, and I saw it wasn't a fight at all. The kids had cornered a little girl. I looked around for a teacher, but no one was in sight.

"Now who is that?" one of the top girls asked.

Then we could see clearly.

"Oh my God," said the Queen. "It's that nasty little Spoon child."

"I can smell her from here," choked one of the ladies.

The smallest Spoon stood in the middle of a circle of kids. Her long hair hung past her elbows, and the hem of her wet dress was tucked like a tail between her legs. She stared at the ground as if the answer to her predicament was written in the dirt.

The kids circled silently. Then all fell back but one. It was Chip, so-called because of his broken front tooth. He was the younger brother of a rough boy: hair bleached white by the southern sun, blue eyes, shirt tail flapping like a bird's broken wing.

All the kids stopped playing to watch.

"Guess he's ready to move up," said the Queen.

Chip had a baseball, and he tossed it gently into the air and caught it with both hands.

Now this boy wasn't that big except in his own mind. He never picked on anyone but the little kids. I could probably shove him aside and grab the little Spoon and run. Sheila might find out, and boy, would she be impressed! But if I got down, the top girls wouldn't invite me back up.

Chip tossed the ball at the little girl, and it landed at her feet. She jumped, and some of the kids laughed.

Maybe he just wanted to scare her.

He ran for the ball. This time he blew on it like dice. He walked around the smallest Spoon as if to find the best angle. She remained silent, arms loosely at her sides, the scraggly hair hiding her face. Every inch of her screamed misery.

"He's really gonna do it this time," said the Queen, leaning forward for a closer look, having so much fun now.

Five minutes on the monkey bars wasn't much, but it was all I had.

So I closed my eyes.

Slap!

"Shit!"

Chip was on the ground, and the middle Spoon girl had the ball. She wound up like a World Series baseball player. The ball sailed over the monkey bars, and over the swings, and over the school yard fence. Everyone said ahhhh like we were watching fireworks. It was magnificent! It was unbelievable! No one had ever seen a girl throw a ball like that before. Then we all heard the delicious tinkling of breaking glass. I leaned over so far to watch; I slipped and fell off the monkey bars.

Thudding hard on the ground, the fall knocked the breath out of me. All I could do was lay there on my back, deflated. Up through the monkey bars, all the top girls stared down at me and giggled. The Queen yawned and turned away.

Slowly, I sat up and looked around. Sheila Spoon had picked up her little sister, snot face, wet dress, and everything. They were disappearing into the back door of the school, and now, carrying the child on her hip, she looked just like a grown woman.

Every now and then my mama, when she was feeling strong and brave, put on her hat and heels and little white gloves and met Spencer and me at the front gate after school, and we all walked home together. Mostly though she didn't like being on the streets since strange men yelled at her from the cabs of their trucks and demanded to know if she wanted to play patty cake. She had tales about women, too, mysterious foreign women who stared at her from behind their kitchen curtains, solemnly stared at her without blinking their eyes. She was filled with kooky stories that she believed, but I didn't. She got lonely without anyone to talk to all day. She had always been shy about visiting with the neighbors and complained they gossiped about her behind her back, which they did, but as I found out on more than one of my snooping expeditions, they did that with everyone. So, just to have something to say, she made up tales After all, she knew we wouldn't be interested in the mopping of the kitchen floor or the making of the unmade bed. But, come to think of it, the silly stories about kidnapped babies and murdered ladies were better than when she didn't talk at all.

On a rare day, Daddy would meet us if he finished his delivery route early and was in a good mood. We'd stop at the Dairy DeLite on the way home. Spencer and me licked ice cream cones while Daddy gambled the grocery money on the pinball machine. Mama fussed when he came to pick us up because sometimes it meant we'd be eating fried potatoes the rest of the week and not much else.

The last bell of the day rang, and I braced myself.

Mama liked pretty clothes. She would understand. I didn't let myself think about how long it had been since she had voted in my favor. If I could talk her into letting me keep the panther, then maybe she could talk Daddy into it. That was the way it worked at our house; it was like praying to the Virgin Mary in order to get a favor from God. I got to the front gate, my mouth was all set for bragging to Spencer, but who was there? It had to be Daddy, still dressed in his work uniform, smoking a Camel. They stood in the crowd of kids that flowed by. Spencer saw me first.

"There's Martha," he yelled, "and she's got a new coat!"

That Spencer and his big mouth.

"Hi, Daddy," I said as if I dressed like a top girl every day.

"Where did you get that coat?" asked Daddy, frowning.

"The principal took me to the clothes closet today." I looked him right in the eyes. "Isn't it beautiful? I think it's panther." I ran my hands down the coat. I touched the collar. "This is real leopard spot."

"I don't care what it is," he said, "Take it off now." He flicked his cigarette to the sidewalk and ground it out with the toe of his shoe.

"But, Daddy, the principal --"

For the second time that day I was pushed toward a door. First me walking fast, then Daddy behind me breathing so hard it parted my hair, and finally, Spencer running to keep up. We went back inside the school and down the hall to the principal's office. Spencer wanted to stop at the boy's bathroom, but Daddy wouldn't hear of it. We passed by Diane Bickerstaff Buck and the top girls who always traveled in a pack. They nudged each other and talked behind their hands. We passed by Chip, who slunk by with his head hung in disgrace. Beat up by a girl, ha-ha. People would remember this day and remind him of it the rest of his sorry life. We passed by the five Spoons, and the middle and the little were still holding on. Daddy shoved me into the principal's office, and she stood there with her purse dangling from her elbow, ready to leave. The late afternoon sun streamed through the office windows and threw our tangled shadows on the floor.

"You the principal?" Daddy asked.

"I am." She smiled, and her eyes were huge behind her glasses. "You must be Martha and Spencer's daddy." She held out her hand for a shake. Daddy hesitated. He wasn't used to shaking hands with no woman, but she didn't back down. He shook once quickly and let go.

"What can I do for you?"

"I thank you, but we can't accept this." Daddy slipped the coat off my shoulders and held it out to her. She didn't take it.

"Martha loves this coat," said the principal. "It was made for her."

"She has her mama's coat," he answered still holding the panther in the empty air.

She still didn't take the panther, and his hand began to sink.

I crossed my arms over my chest and thought about my mama's old coat nestled in the cardboard box. In that moment, I would have been glad for it.

Spencer was jumping up and down. The principal glanced at him as if his fidgeting offended her. Instantly, he froze on one foot. I saw what she saw. Spencer was a street urchin, a boy beggar. We should set him out on the corner with some pencils and a tin cup.

Daddy still held out the coat.

She still wasn't taking it.

So there we were like players in a game of freeze tag: my daddy, dirty and tired from a hard day's work, and the principal woman, all uptown, Spencer and me, two fools.

Then little brother broke the spell.

"Daddy!" He crossed his legs. "I have to go to the bathroom!"

Suddenly, our daddy remembered who he was and began to manifest. He tossed the coat on a chair. "Let's go, kids." He spun around and followed his nose out of the room.

Later that evening at dinner, Daddy, working his way through every bite of food on the table, told how he had saved our honor. He told more than once. He wiggled his ears at the climactic moments. Mama was having one of her quiet days and spent her time playing with a loose curl that had escaped from her hairdo. He didn't seem to notice.

"This one," he pointed at me and I shrank an inch, "this one met us at the schoolhouse door wearing that damn coat!"

Spencer nodded, clearly enjoying the part he had played in the great drama.

Mama came back from whatever planet she was visiting and picked up her fork.

"Did you hear what I said, Pixie? She was wearing the coat!" Daddy helped himself to his third piece of cornbread.

"Martha," Mama paused, fork halfway to her mouth, "you know better."

By the time Daddy pushed back from the table and lit a Camel, he was huge, and I was so small my feet no longer reached the floor. I had been mean to Shelby, my only friend. I had passed up a chance to make a good impression on Sheila Spoon. I had fallen off the monkey bars, and I was sure that my underpants had showed. Now my old coat was laid to rest in a cardboard box, and I knew I would be too scared to ask for her back. I had been a Paris regular for only a short moment, the kind of girl who knew what the Eiffel Tower looked like, spring, summer, fall and winter. Now I knew nothing, and I was so small I needed a stepladder to get down from my chair. My father enjoyed embarrassing me while my mother took her meals on planet Pluto. I would leave this crazy house the second the law allowed. How many more years was that?

Chapter Three
Daffodils, 1970

That year, spring hadn't been able to make up her mind about when she'd show. It'd warm up to seventy degrees, and the winter clothes would get packed away. The old people would start setting out flats of tomatoes and marigolds in the backyard mud. Then the temperature would drop to below freezing, and all the new green leaves would die. It was on a false spring day like that when a visitor came to our house.

Daddy was making a distant delivery in his truck and wouldn't be back until late Saturday. Mama sat on the porch steps smoking from a pack of his Camels, and I sat beside her. Spencer posed on the broken sidewalk with his eyes scrunched and his collar turned up, singing rock and roll into a Popsicle stick. Sweet Pea, a yellow dog with a spot of white on her head, cocked her head and listened, sometimes howling along with the chorus. I threw pebbles at them, but when Spencer ran out of breath, Mama politely applauded.

"I ain't finished yet," he complained.

Just then a small woman drove up in a huge car with fins. She aimed for the curb in front of our house. The front tire came up on the sidewalk, and the rear stuck out in the street. Her hair took up all the space between the top of her head and the roof of the car, so I knew she had something to do with those three old birds back in the country. The woman opened the car door and put one high heel on the pavement. I recognized her then.

She lived a few blocks from here in the neighborhood under the freeway, and she had quite a story. Her husband died and left her a widow. She didn't mourn for long, though. Soon she became a known regular on Saturday nights at Tommy Trent's Fun Barn. All the married women in the neighborhood clucked their tongues and shook their heads whenever her name was mentioned. Then a big change happened. A traveling revival set up a tent across the river, and the sinner came back with her slate wiped clean. Now the women complained because this woman had the audacity to set up her own church, like a man might do.

The lady got out of the car and stood on the sidewalk, a bunch of golden daffodils in one hand. She smoothed her dress, a plain blue cotton one, belted at the waist, like all the housewives wore, but on her feet was a different story. A pair of shiny black pumps with heels so high and thin to wear them was to defy the laws of gravity. Spencer admired her fins, but Mama and me watched those Frederick's of Hollywood heels come tapping up the sidewalk.

Mama didn't talk to strangers, and everybody knew it. When we were younger if an unexpected knock fell on the door, Mama grabbed us, and we hid in the closet until the danger passed. I was in third grade before I figured out we weren't playing hide-and-seek. One day when a knock came, I knew, just like that, it wasn't a game. Mama was scared. I wasn't. So I stayed put, sitting in the living room floor playing with my dolls. I refused to budge even though Mama whispered, "hurry up hurry up," and pushed Spencer into the closet. Then the knock came again, and it was a timid tapping, not the confident knock of a pushy salesman or the knock of a neighbor who needed to borrow seventy-five cents. So that day I stood up.

"I'm going to see who it is," I had said.

A muffled moan came from inside the closet.

"It's okay," I reassured the door and walked over to the front window and pushed the curtain aside.

It was only Shelby, who lived a few blocks away. He saw me and mouthed the words, "Can you play?"

I nodded and dropped the curtain.

"It's Shelby." I told the closet door.

No answer.

"You know Shelby. He's my age."

The closet door gave me the cold shoulder.

"He has red hair," I said, hoping for a sign of recognition.

Still no answer.

"I'm going to go outside and play."

Later when I came back inside, everything had slipped back to normal. My dolls were right where I left them. Spencer watched cartoons, and Mama stood at the kitchen sink peeling potatoes. She never got me back in the closet again. I started answering the door all the time, and soon it became my official job to deal with whoever was standing there, good news or bad. I don't know what Mama did when I wasn't home. I did not like to think about her hiding in the closet among the musty old clothes and boxes of broken things, staring big-eyed into the darkness. The closet seemed scarier to me than living out in the free world. I took my chances. A knock at the door could mean trouble, but it might be your friend asking you to come outside and play.

"How y'all this evening?" the intruder asked. "I'm Sister Thelma, pastor of God's House of Whole Truth. Y'all probably know where that is, don't cha?"

She was old, at least thirty or forty. She shook our hands and patted Sweet Pea on the head, as smooth and friendly as a politician right before election day. The church she spoke of was close by. Sooner or later, it sucked in all the sinners in the neighborhood, especially sinners who had just lost their job or their wits. It lit up on Saturday nights with singing and clapping coming from inside.

Mama watched the sidewalk and ground out her cigarette. I knew she didn't want the woman to get a close look at her bruised face.

"My cousin from the Holy Ghost Temple just made her annual visit. She told me I should call on you," Sister Thelma said.

Which one was her cousin: the Bowling Ball, the Big Bosom, or the Tambourine?

Sister Thelma offered the daffodils to Mama. "These are for you," she said, "from my yard."

Mama slowly looked up and accepted the flowers. She hid her face in them. Their fresh perfume floated on the air. "I been wishing someone would come by," Mama said to the daffodils.

"You want to hear me sing?" asked Spencer.

"You don't want to hear him sing," I told the lady.

She smiled at us, each one of us, and this time her smile was so warm and genuine, it made the weak sun brighter.

Sweet Pea licked her hand.

"Who got that paint on you?" She pretended to wipe away the spot of white on the dog's head.

"She lives next door," I said.

The lady nodded.

"But she likes us best," said Spencer.

And to prove it, Sweet Pea trotted over to Spencer and nudged him with her nose.

Mama stood up.

"Would you like to come in?" she asked.

Saturday evening found Spencer and me at the supper table. We had just finished up the fried potatoes, pinto beans, and cornbread. Spencer was licking his plate just to aggravate me. I pointed my butter knife at him.

"Die, commoner," I said in my best Queen of England voice.

We were going to the Holy Roller church that night. Would Sheila Spoon be there? One day at school I told her we were paying a visit to God's House of Whole Truth, and she had looked up from the book she was reading long enough to say politely, "*oh really?*" Then she went right back to doing her work.

Every afternoon I collected empty pop bottles. When I had a sack full, I was going to cash them in for a bag of penny candy. Maybe we could get something started over a bag of Atomic Fire Balls. Maybe I'd see her at the church tonight, and we could sit together.

Had Sheila ever been to the ocean? If we were best friends, I bet she'd go with me. We could get jobs waiting tables or hire out on a fishing boat. We could sail anywhere in the world. While we decided if it would be Hong Kong or Paris, we'd take barefoot walks, smell the clean salt air, eat fried shrimp from a paper plate every day. No one in my family had ever eaten shrimp, although Daddy had a long boring story about clams.

Mama, who had gone into her bedroom to get dressed for church, walked back into the kitchen.

"Ta- da!" She turned in a circle. "How do I look?"

Mama wore her wedding dress that I had only seen in pictures. Where had she been hiding it? It was satiny white and went all the way to the floor. Peeking out from underneath were her pink bedroom slippers. The dress had been handmade for Mama when she younger and still had all her baby fat, and now it hung off her shoulders like it was still on the hanger. A little hat nested in her hair, and a net came down and covered half her face.

"It's very nice," I lied.

"It'll be yours someday."

"Oh, boy," I answered. "I can't wait."

"You look like a fairy princess, Mama," said Spencer, batting his big cowlashes.

She walked over and kissed him on his little greasy mouth. They were a sweet couple.

I stood up and started stacking the dirty dishes. "But what are you going to wear to church?"

"I'm wearing this." She smoothed the skirt of her dress.

I froze right there with the bean juice dripping off my fingers.

"No."

"Yes." Mama smiled like a woman who had just won the Pick Seven.

"Why?"

"It's the nicest thing I have."

"It's your wedding dress."

Mama twirled around like a little girl. "I don't care."

"But, Mama, it's not right!"

"It is right," she answered. "It's the perfect choice."

I finally had a chance to see Sheila Spoon outside the classroom, and my mother was going to embarrass me to death.

"It'll look great with that bruise on your face," I said

Spencer jumped out of his chair and started kicking me. I held him off with one hand until Mama pulled him away.

Why oh why oh why did I have to have this family?

"Finish the dishes," she said, "then you get ready." She turned and left the room, dragging Spencer with her, while he threw dirty looks over his shoulder. She always walked on the backs of her slippers, and I noticed her crusty heels. Good Lord, what was Sheila Spoon going to think?

"Hey, are you sure you want to go to church?" I yelled after her. "You won't know anyone there. They'll all be strangers!"

"Get ready," came from the other room.

Spencer slicked his hair back with Vitalis and stuffed a fresh wad of Juicy Fruit into his mouth. I pulled on a pair of clean jeans and my sneakers and wore some of Mama's Baby Rose lipstick. All that time, I plotted a way to make it look like I wasn't with the bride. When we set off down the broken sidewalk for God's House of Whole Truth, I lingered behind. The church used to be the neighborhood grocery store, but the river flooded and the people with money fled. Now the Holy Rollers rented it out.

Sweet Pea ran out of her yard when we passed by and kept us company until Mama yelled and hurt her feelings. Some of the streetlights were out, and we tripped in the dark. Boarded up buildings stared at us with empty faces. I walked a half block behind my family until a man with whiskers walked out of the shadows and smacked his lips at me. Heart pounding, I ran until I was almost standing on the back of Mama's skirt. We turned a corner, and there it was, all lit up, with a big sign out front that shouted: JESUS WANTS YOU!!!! Mama caught her breath, and her hand went to her heart. The light poured out of the building's storefront windows and seemed to shine right on her. She looked dazzled. From inside the church came singing: *Call Him up/call Him up/tell Him what you want/Jesus on the mainline now.*

I decided to pretend that I went to church every Saturday night with a woman dressed in a wedding gown. As we climbed the steps, I practiced my snob look: eyebrows raised, nose in the air, mouth turned down at the corners. Mama pushed the door open, and the three of us walked in together. The people kept right on singing. It looked like a normal church, pulpit and altar up front, folding metal chairs. Two wooden boards hung on each side of the pulpit, one signifying Sunday School attendance (seven) and the other announcing the offering (two dollars and twenty-three cents). Mama watched her feet as we edged along the wall toward the back. The rotten smell of dead fishies rose up to greet us, and I remembered the flood. Spencer pinched his nose until Mama saw and pushed his hand away. How old would we have to be before we could say "that stinks" about something that stank?

The sight of the five Spoon sisters all sitting together made me forget the question. The girls were arranged according to size with their parents like bookends. They were five rows down.

Quickly, I lowered my nose.

Three rows down. Sheila Spoon looked up, glanced at Mama, glanced at me.

I slapped my face with a smile.

Sheila lifted her chin in the air.

It was half of a nod.

If we could get out of the church without anyone throwing rice at Mama, maybe this wouldn't be so bad after all.

We sat down behind the Spoons in the back row. They called this spot in the church Sinner's Alley, but I wouldn't learn this that night. Sister Thelma, accompanied by her Godzilla hair, played a wheezy old accordion up front. People clapped and sang. There was an old grandma keeping time with a cane. A boy tied in a wheelchair wagging his head from side to side. The bum who lived in the train tunnel stretched out napping. No one seemed the least surprised to see Mama in her wedding dress, so I relaxed. The song ended, and Sister

Thelma asked for a volunteer to come forward for the Children's Moment. The littlest Spoon went up and sang *Jesus loves me this I know* while Sister Thelma played softly on her accordion. Everybody applauded, and the little Spoon ducked her head. Then Sister Thelma laid the accordion in its case and got down to business. I checked her out. Dusty black dress like something your old maid aunt would wear to her own funeral. She began pacing back and forth, so I got a good look at the feet. This time - shiny red pumps, very Dorothy and Toto. Not nearly as foxy as the black ones she wore to our house but still out of place.

"Is there anyone here tonight who needs a blessing from the Lord?" she asked. "Anything you'd like to come and lay at this here altar? I'm telling you tonight, brothers and sisters, Jesus can take it from you."

The old grandma heaved herself up. Using her cane, she slowly made her way down the aisle. She stopped in front of the altar.

"I need to be healed," she cried. "I need to be healed of my affliction."

"God can cause you to lay aside that cane," said Sister Thelma. "Are you ready to give it up?"

"No," said the grandma, "it ain't the cane. I got the sugar diabetes."

Sister Thelma's face flushed. "God can take the cane *and* the sugar diabetes." She shouted and pounded the pulpit. "I said, are you ready to be healed?" For a small person, she had a really loud voice.

"Yes," the old woman cried, "oh, yes, Jesus, take it from me."

Everyone raised their arms and began to pray. Spencer slid down in his seat, but I wasn't scared. It was just talking to God. The people got louder as if they thought God was hard of hearing. Spencer tugged on

Mama's sleeve, but she wouldn't look at him. She just sat there hypnotized.

I elbowed Spencer in the side.

"Look," I whispered. On the wall hung a picture of Jesus, the one of him with the sad, chocolate eyes. Underneath the picture was a hole with some writing scratched over it.

"What does it say?" asked Spencer.

"Cockroach Motel," I read. "No Vacancy."

As if he'd been listening, a cockroach poked his head out of the hole. His feelers swept the air. Spencer leaned forward for a closer look and forgot he was afraid of the loud people. Up front, Sister Thelma started up again.

"Now I say to you tonight, brothers and sisters, come to the altar before it is too late. For it is written, He will return in the twinkling of an eye and take his followers home. Won't you come now and give your soul to the Lord?"

We could see the cockroach hadn't figured out if he wanted to commit. He crawled a little ways out of the Motel, then turned and ran back in. A second later he popped out again. This time his mind was made up. He ran down the wall, up the center aisle, and all the way to the front of the church. Spencer and me cracked up, and he dropped his wad of Juicy Fruit. Mama came out of her coma and gave us a look. We were about to get in trouble.

But Mama lifted the net from her face and pinned it to her hat, patting it softly. She slid to the edge of her chair. Suddenly, she was all lit up, and for a moment, it was like she had become something other than a kooky woman wearing a wedding dress in a fish gut storefront church. Somehow she had taken on the look of a woman who was important, like a woman you read about in a magazine. I had never seen her look this way before. Mama rose from her chair and walked down the aisle.

Her pink slippers went whack, whack, whack on the floor. A great shout of praise went out from the people.

Spencer forgot he was cured from thumb sucking and popped the right one in his mouth.

I squirmed in my seat.

How could my mama change like that? I had turned my head to look at a bug, and when I turned it back, she was someone different. How could she change like that while she was sitting right beside me? What had happened to her, anyway?

Sister Thelma and the Holy Rollers gathered around Mama, and we couldn't see her anymore. They raised their hands to the ceiling once again. Sheila Spoon turned around.

"Hey," she said.

"Hey," I said back. "What's this all about?"

"She's getting saved."

"Saved from what?"

"You'll see."

A little while later, Mama was helped back to her chair with her hat crooked and mascara smeared down to her chin. Someone handed her a handkerchief, and she wiped her face. Then she gave a big sigh and settled back like something was finished. Mama turned and smiled at me and Spencer as if to say everything was a-okay.

I felt completely baffled. Mama had put on her wedding dress, and she had marched us down to the storefront church. She had volunteered to go up front. She let strangers put their hands on her. I wasn't used to Mama making *decisions.* Woman, I thought, what has happened to you?

Thoughtfully, I rubbed my chin. Maybe this was a clear case of an *Invasion of the Body Snatchers.* Last night while my real mother had slept, her foamy seed pod sprouted. Now this imposter lived in her place. Was I going to have to stab her with a pitchfork? Man, I needed a stiff drink. Spencer looked at me with question marks in his eyes, but I couldn't tell him anything. He coughed politely into his hand. I stared at the holes in my sneakers and waited for what would happen next.

The daddy of the Spoon girls spoke up.

"I have something I need to bring to the attention of this church," he said.

"Tell it, Brother Spoon," everyone cried.

"Tell it, Brother Spoon," my mama echoed.

The Spoon daddy reached with the longest arm I'd ever seen and took hold of his middle daughter, my classmate.

"We're going up front." He pulled Sheila down the aisle. The little Spoon jumped up and grabbed her sister's skirt. The daddy didn't like it, and he turned around and looked at his wife. I imagined them communicating telepathically:

Remove that thing, Igor.

Yes, Master.

The mama pulled the little girl back.

At the front of the church, Sheila jammed her hands in her skirt pockets and found something on the floor to stare at. Poor Sheila. The daddy put his arm over her shoulders.

"This one," he said and gave her a squeeze. "The devil is trying to take this one from me." He raised his hand high in the sky. "Lord, I can't let that happen!" He yelled and stomped his foot.

Spencer and me jumped. The old grandma cried out. The little Spoon crawled into her mother's lap. The bum who lived in the train tunnel woke up from his nap. The boy tied in the wheelchair wagged his head from side to side.

"She slipped past my chair last night carrying the radio and went in the bathroom and locked the door. I called for Sister Spoon. I said, 'Mother, come here and see what your middle daughter is doing.' Mother peeked through the keyhole, then jumped back. She said, 'You better look, Father.' I looked. That girl was standing on the toilet moving her hips to the beat of the devil's music."

All the grown-ups shook their heads sadly. Even Mama.

Sheila Spoon glanced up then, and our eyes met. Her face turned red, and she quickly looked down at the floor again. Even her hairy black eyebrows looked sad and defeated. I felt so sorry I was seeing this. Then right in front of my eyes, the middle Spoon made a miraculous u-turn. She looked up at me again, and this time, she glared! She stuck her jaw in the air, and it was as strong and pretty as the jawbone of an ass. A magnificent comeback!

Suddenly, I was riding in a falling elevator. My stomach went all queasy. I touched my forehead to see if I had a sudden temperature. It was then that I understood that every moment before this one had been as ordinary as a fried baloney sandwich.

I had just left friendship behind and jumped right into l-o-v-e, love.

But her daddy wasn't done with her yet. He shouted and held fast. "But that was not all that this girl did. Oh no, that is not all. My daughter had tooken off her clothes, and she was dancing in her underpants!"

A death moan rose up from the church.

"Mama!" I whispered. "He shouldn't be telling this!"

"Hush, Martha," she answered. "That's the way they do it here."

Sister Thelma spoke up.

"This child is demon possessed. We must put ourselves in one mind and one accord and cast the demons out."

Like the moment before a tornado hit, all fell silent, the sky turned dark at midday, and the wind. You knew it was time to head to the storm cellar, if you were lucky enough to have one, or a four-clawed bathtub, if you weren't. People left their seats and went to Brother Spoon and his middle daughter. Mama lowered her head, but I could see her peeking. She rubbed the satin of her skirt and rocked back and forth. Spencer buried his head in my side, and I put my arm around him. The leftover Spoons went into a huddle. The boy tied in the wheelchair wagged his head from side to side. The bum who lived in the train tunnel must have decided it was safer at home for he ran out the door.

The Holy Rollers put their hands on Sheila: the top of her head, her shoulders, her arms, her back. They pushed; they pulled. They jerked her this way and that. Their prayers rose up and hovered over her like a storm cloud. Lightning flashed and thunder rolled. Tears fell like rain. Brother Spoon began to shuffle his feet and swing his arms, a kind of dance that was allowed, I guessed. The old grandma danced the same dance and made watery footprints on the wooden floor.

Then Sister Thelma cried out.

"Are you clean now, child? Are you clean?"

Sheila Spoon stood proud. She raised her head higher and higher and stared at something no one else could see. I didn't want to witness anymore, but I couldn't turn away.

"Bring me the bottle of healing oil!" said Sister Thelma. She poured some oil on her handkerchief and put it to Sheila's forehead. Later I learned that this oil was reserved for special hard cases, like a woman who wanted to divorce her husband or someone with a large tumor.

The prayers continued.

"Are you clean now, child?"

Still no answer.

Sister Thelma uncapped the bottle of oil and poured it on top of Sheila's head. It dripped down her face. She didn't even blink. Say you're clean, I pleaded, go ahead and get it over with.

"Come out of this child, you malignant son of Satan!" commanded Sister Thelma.

Daddy Spoon went down like someone hit him in the head. He rolled over on his back and didn't move. The old grandma fell out like a tree crashing in the woods. Spencer started crying and hid his face in my lap. I looked at Mama willing her to do *something*, but she kept rocking.

"Are you clean now, child?"

Nothing. Not a sound.

The little Spoon broke her mother's grasp and ran out in the aisle. She clenched her fists and yelled.

"Say you're clean, Sissy, say you're clean so we can just go home!"

Brother Spoon heard. He sat up like Dracula rising from his coffin at the crack of dusk. He started pushing himself up.

Sister Spoon jerked the smallest daughter back to safety. The little girl howled.

All of this got Sheila's attention. She moved her eyes from the water stains on the ceiling and looked sadly at her baby sister.

"I'm clean," she said so quietly my heart broke for her.

"What did you say?" Sister Thelma asked.

"I. Am. Clean."

"Hallelujah!" everyone cried, and they all broke into a chorus of *Victory in Jesus.*

That night Mama walked home with her head in the clouds, and the forecast never changed. Spencer and I followed at her heels and didn't fight at all. Back home, she quickly wiggled out of her wedding dress and stuck it in the back of the closet. Still hours passed before we heard Daddy's car out front. We all paused and sniffed the air. Spencer and I sat down at the kitchen table, and Mama took Daddy's plate out of the oven. This night Daddy's footsteps were slow and heavy on the floor, the walk of a worn-out man. Somehow he knew, though, we'd been up to something.

Daddy asked, "Where the hell were y'all tonight?"

"At God's House of Whole Truth," Mama answered him.

"So you turning into a Holy Roller now, Pixie?" he asked.

"That nice Sister Thelma came by and personally invited us all to church. Wasn't that sweet of her?"

"Sister Thelma?" Daddy snorted. "That old whore that used to hold up the wall at Tommy Trent's?"

Usually Mama ducked her head right about now, but this time she stayed steady. "Sister Thelma gave all that up," she explained.

All except for the high heels, I thought.

Then Daddy sat down at the kitchen table and leaned back in his chair.

"Now let me get this straight," he began and his voice traveled all over the room.

Sister Thelma's daffodils, in a jelly jar filled with water, decorated the table, but he didn't notice them. At the sound of his voice, their yellow heads drooped lower and lower.

Mama brought him a bowl of the beans from the back burner. He scraped the food into his mouth like he hadn't eaten in days and sopped up the brown juice with white bread.

"Let me get this straight," he said again when he caught his breath. "She's a reformed whore now?"

A few of the daffodils drooped so low, they slid out of the jar and landed on the table.

Mama ignored the question. She picked up the daffodils and put them back in the water.

"Why were you so late?" she asked.

"Somebody's got to make a living in this family," he answered. He went back to scraping his plate.

"Is that right?" Mama said.

"Is there something you want to say, Pixie?"

We all waited to see if there was something she wanted to say.

Mama's silence hung in the air and shimmered quietly there.

I propped my elbows on the table and rested my head in my hands. When I closed my eyes, I saw proud Sheila Spoon standing in front of the church with all those hands poking and prodding her. I saw my mama lit up like the sun. And here was Daddy halfheartedly trying to pick a fight. I wanted to nudge him and say, "Something happened to your wife tonight, old man. Better watch out."

No more was said about God's House of Whole Truth or where Daddy had been so late. He got up from the table and helped himself to more beans from the stove. Spencer crawled under the kitchen table and sucked his thumb, and with the other hand, he held on to Mama's foot. I left the room and crawled in my bed and put the covers over my head where I had a bad dream about cockroaches and train tunnels and wedding dresses. It was all mixed up.

Chapter Four

Rainbows for Jesus, 1970

The kids in my neighborhood always loved spring cleaning. It began when one housewife wrestled open winter-stuck windows. Then another threw her rugs over the clothesline and beat them without mercy. It was as if all the women felt a strange vibration because by the end of the day, every house was turned upside down. Mothers dragged boxes of trash and other good junk into the alley for the garbage man who didn't come until Friday. That gave us plenty of time to go from pile to pile scrounging for loot. It was like a free day for kids and the usual laws among us did not apply. Shelby put on a torn skirt and swished down the alley. No one beat him up. A girl wore an old blue work shirt with Freddy stitched in cursive letters over the front pocket. *Hand me that wrench*, she said in a deep voice, and pretended to fix a flat. *Honey, time for supper*, a boy in a house dress sang in a sweet voice, and we all fell out. Sweet Pea, the neighbor man's dog, jumped for joy, and Spencer fit a little girl's torn Easter bonnet on her head and tied the sash under her chin. Instead of shaking it off like a regular dog, she pranced down the dirty alley as if she herself had rolled away the stone. We took what we wanted and didn't worry about the trash that spilled onto the ground. Later, our mothers came outside for a breath of fresh air and found unmentionables scattered up and down the street for the whole world to see. Some of the women wised up and started burning the stuff.

My mama forgot about the spring cleaning that year. When we came home from school, we were never assaulted with the smell of her special cleaning brew made of ammonia and vinegar and rocket fuel. We were never locked outside for hours because she had just got down on her hands and knees and waxed and buffed the floor. One Saturday afternoon when the cool of spring was over and the heat of summer had already begun, she started carrying out things to the blackened spot in the backyard. She had finally gotten around to the ritual burn. I left the book I was reading to go and see.

It wasn't quite that.

Spencer was already there. He had a bucket of water in case the fire got out of control. One year it did and almost took out the neighbor man's tool shed. Today the fire burned bright and flying ashes filled the warm air. Mama was feeding it her collection of movie magazines. The flames licked the pages, like a child licking a lollipop. I stood with my hands in the pockets of my blue jeans and watched for awhile.

"Seven times hotter," Mama said.

She quoted stuff like that all the time now. Sometimes I could figure out what she meant. I wasn't ignorant. I knew all about Adam and Eve and the Serpent, Jonah and the Big Fish, Daniel in the Lion's Den, all those stories. Once when I was a little kid, I had played one of the three wise kings in the Christmas play at school. Shoot, around here you'd have to live under a rock not to know about Jesus since only the liquor stores outnumbered the churches. But what Mama said these days came straight from God's House of Whole Truth, and those people were jammed up and jelly tight.

She reached into the shoe box which held her makeup. A tube of blood red lipstick. She threw it in and fire met fire. A powder puff. The little brush she used to put on eye shadow. Mama had kept her good mood for a long time after the night of her salvation. The next time we went to church, she had gotten fixed up and put on pink, blue, and green eye shadow. Of course, Daddy was out of town. She fluttered her eyelids for Spencer and me and declared she was wearing *Rainbows for Jesus!* We thought it funny until after the service. Sister Thelma told her it was a sin to wear make-up. She went over to the shelf where they kept the hymnals and the offering basket and took down the thickest book I had ever seen. Sister Thelma thumbed through it. There it is, she said, rule number six hundred and thirty-seven: Thou shalt be modest from your head to your ankles. Mama nodded, all shame-faced, and said, "*I had forgotten that.*"

"Seven times hotter," Mama muttered again.

We heard a lot about sin. Sin and four-legged animals. Mama said sin was always waiting to reach out and grab you. She didn't want us to end up at the left hand of Jesus with the goats, the bleating goats who would be herded straight into the devil's barbecue pit on judgment day. Mama wanted us to stand at the right hand of Jesus with the sheep, the curly sheep who would hoof it down the streets of gold and pick out their own palaces. Mama convinced Spencer that holy rolling was the way to go. At one prayer meeting he had answered the altar call, and every night since they sat on the sofa like Siamese twins reading from the Bible.

Spencer probably wasn't sincere. He might be pulling a sneaky trick in order to get all Mama's attention and be called her "little lover man" or "angel baby." He had always been a mama's boy. But he had stopped singing rock and roll songs, and he'd loved them. Now he dominated the Children's Moment at Whole Truth on Saturday nights.

I didn't care if they left me out, and to prove it, when Bible study started on the couch, I'd turn the radio on as loud as it would go and put on a show. Singing and dancing always gave me an appetite, so then it'd be time to make popcorn on the stove. I hadn't really meant to drop the pan and the lid and everything on the floor that one time, but it sure did get Mama off the couch in a hurry.

Now where was Daddy when all this was going on? Most nights he worked late and came home in time to eat supper and fall in bed. He'd be gone again before we got up. Mama didn't dare preach to him like she did to Spencer and me. Every now and then Daddy went to church with us. Just to keep an eye on things, he said. Everybody welcomed him and called him "Brother Charlie" even though he never came close to answering the altar call. Mama acted like a normal person on those nights, although she would still sing the songs and raise her hands in prayer. Daddy would crack jokes on the drive home and pretend to pray to the Father, the Son, and the Holy Goat. He did a bad imitation of the old grandma who always carried a cane and a spit can. We had stepped out of the church late one night and surprised her while she stood in the shadows. She had one foot on the curb and one foot on the street. Her long skirts covered everything, except the sound of her pee hitting the concrete. I had never seen a woman pee standing up before, and I couldn't wait to try it myself. Daddy joked about her all the way home in a way that was so mean, nobody laughed. I don't think he realized how far gone Mama was. This wasn't a joke to her. Daddy hardly believed that she could want something for herself or that it would last more than a minute. All she had ever done was clean house and fix herself up and wait for Daddy to come home. And now that she had gotten saved, something new erupted every day. So usually I kept my nose in my book and stayed away from her and Spencer.

Back at the fire, she picked up her sundress and tossed it in, her pretty red sundress that earned a wolf whistle from Daddy anytime she wore it. I always loved that dress because she acted sassy when she had it on. The fire turned blue and burned the dress. I turned blue for a moment, too, but I wiped the feeling away and watched it go up in smoke. When I turned eighteen, I told myself, I'm leaving home. I'm going to live on the beach. I will never feel sad again.

Next she threw in a pair of shorts.

The greedy fire roared its approval. Something popped inside and threw a spark across the yard. Spencer doused it with a little water from his bucket.

"Now your turn, Spencer."

He had a small pile of stuff at his feet. He threw a tattered poster in the fire, Elvis doing a dance number from *Jailhouse Rock*. Next it was his collection of Superman and Green Hornet comic books. A few baseball cards. Spencer hadn't been a big sinner. He walked over to Mama, and she pulled him to her.

"Good boy," she said, stroking his hair. They watched the fire demolish Spencer's earthly treasures. His thumb hovered around his mouth, but at the last second, it scratched his ear instead.

I looked around. Nothing of Daddy's waited to feed the fire. Our little television and the radio still camped out in the living room. Well, she's crazy, I thought, but at least she ain't stupid.

"Hell will be seven times hotter than this here fire, Martha."

"That's pretty hot, Mama." Our eyes met. Another sermon began to rise. Cross my legs at the knee instead of the ankle. Be a good little Christian girl. Go to the altar. Make her proud. Like Spencer.

She pushed hair off of her forehead. She didn't have a bowling ball yet, but with the can of Aqua Net, she could manage a grapefruit.

I backed away from the fire until my heels hit the door steps. "Think I'll go take a bath now. Get ready for church." I gave her a fake smile and escaped inside.

The bathtub slowly filled with hot water. I kicked my dirty clothes off and left them in the floor. Ahhh, the water felt good. I liked being the first one, not having to bathe in anyone else's gray soapy water. The steam would make my mousy hair curl a little, too, which was always a bonus. Mama said I had curls all over my head when I was born. She favored naturally curly hair. Once she had told stories about when I was a baby and how she felt when they put me in her arms in the hospital. Instant love, she had always said, like instant pudding. She didn't tell stories about me like that anymore. I was too old for baby stories anyway. I tightened my jaw into the jawbone of an ass.

I lay back in the tub and closed my eyes. Church was tonight and that always brought Sheila to mind. My efforts at winning her affections had taken a tumble. Since her humiliation at Whole Truth, she wouldn't even look at me and never offered a "hey." I tried passing her a note in school, but she handed it to the kid sitting next to her, not even noticing it had *Sheila Spoon* written on it in my best cursive. A paper sack of Atomic Fire Balls would not be enough. Thinking about her always made me feel good and soon I started singing, using the soap for a microphone.

"My ba-bee does the hank-y pank-y." My voice rose up with the steam, filling the small bathroom, and shutting out the backyard craziness. I didn't know any more words to the song, so I sang that part probably a hundred times. I wasn't sure exactly what the hanky panky was, but I knew it was nasty. Did Sheila Spoon know how to do the hanky panky? I closed my eyes so I could get a better picture of all this, occasionally turning the hot on with my big toe when the water got cold.

I invited Sheila to come to my little party. She walked out of the steam and smiled at me. Then she slid out of her homely dress and slipped into the bathtub, leaned toward me and put her lips on mine.

I about died.

She laughed out loud at my surprise.

I had never heard her laugh before.

"I've liked you all this time," she said, touching my cheek, smoothing my hair.

In spite of the hot bath water, I shivered.

"You are one stone fox, Martha."

Me? Stone fox? Blonde Marsha Brady was a stone fox. The skinny sister on the Partridge family was a stone fox. She could sing, too. I was plain old Martha.

"Wrong," Sheila said, reading my thoughts.

I wanted to touch her, too, but I was afraid I'd make her disappear.

"Go ahead," she said.

Then something happened. A noise. Startled, I sat up straight in the bathtub with my arms across my chest. Sheila dived under the water. No one was there, but my clothes were missing from the bathroom floor. A stupid Spencer trick. He was always messing everything up for me. Curses!

I wrapped myself in the towel and went into the bedroom. Out the window, Mama and Spencer still fed the fire. I opened my dresser drawer to get a fresh pair of jeans. The drawer was empty! I slammed it and opened another one. Empty again. I yanked open the closet. Only the usual dresses worn to school or when my life was threatened hung limp from the hangers. I put on my nightgown and went outside.

The fire was even bigger and hotter than before.

"Mama, Spencer came in while I was taking a bath and took my clothes. My jeans are missing out of my drawer." I turned to him. "What kind of stupid trick is this?"

"We heard you singing." He poked the fire with a stick.

"So what?"

"It's a sin to sing dirty songs."

I thought about taking the stick away and whacking him with it, but the time was not right. I would deal with him later.

"Mama, make him give me my clothes back. I need to get dressed."

"I sent him inside to get your jeans."

"Why?" I asked.

"Look in your closet. All your dresses are hanging there."

"I don't want a dress. I want to wear my jeans. What did you do with them?"

"Martha, are you dense? What do you think I'm doing with them?"

I glanced at the fire. And looked again. And looked again. My jeans were burning! They hissed and spit and cried for me. My blue jeans!

I grabbed the bucket of water and threw it on the fire. I dragged a smoking pair out and stomped the cha-cha-cha on it with my bare feet. It whimpered; then it was dead. I screamed bloody murder.

"Help me get the rest out!"

Mama and Spencer stood there and watched, their faces blank.

I grabbed the bucket of water from Spencer and attacked the fire. Smoke rose up, choking me. I drank a gallon of it, staggering around in a circle. I had to back away or pass out.

"How could you do this?" I yelled at Mama.

"You're going to wear dresses from now on. I can't have you running around here looking no better than one of them pagan Catholics." Mama set her mouth in a grim line.

Spencer did the same thing, like he knew the horrors of being a pagan Catholic.

"Mama, please, help me get them out. I can't climb a tree in a dress. All the kids will laugh at me." I dragged another pair out of the fire, but they were already gone.

"Leave them alone, Martha. I said you ain't wearing them no more." She picked the jeans up with a stick and threw them back into the flames.

I saw them curl up...a pocket, a hem, a hole in the knee, a leg shaped like mine, a bone.

"All the kids will laugh at me, Mama," I pleaded. I knew she could understand how that felt.

She drew herself up to her full height of five-feet one-and-a-half inches. "You be glad when the kids laugh. They laughed at Jesus, too, and He died on the cross for you."

Hot tears ran down my face. I smeared them off. My grandma would have never done anything like this. She didn't worry herself about Jesus and all his stupid rules. Her god was the god who loved people and gave them extravagant gifts like lightning bugs on a summer night or dimples on a fat baby's butt. My grandma thought Jesus was sorry.

"Your Jesus," I said, "your Jesus can kiss my big toe."

Then I turned calmly away with the dignity of a grown-up woman.

I ended up in church that night with her fingerprints on my cheek, a busted lip, a blister on my foot, and wearing a scratchy little girl dress with a pink ruffle. It was so sickening sweet only a Blondie would have worn it to her ninety-nine-year-old grandma's birthday party. Mama had time to let down the hem, and the dress banged my ankles. All the sheep women stared at me when I walked in and elbowed their buddies. They smiled at Mama and nodded their approval. I swear she grew a half-inch taller right in front of my eyes

I sat down, eyes straight ahead. You could buy jeans for fifty cents a pair at the Salvation Army, and I had the money.

Daddy came along this time, his head drooping before the service started. He didn't know about the burning in the back yard, or he wouldn't have been napping so peacefully. Maybe I'd tell him. He'd kill her for burning stuff he had to work so hard to pay for.

Sister Thelma commandeered the pulpit. Tonight her hair swirled on her head like an ice cream cone. I knew she had to bend her knees to see the whole thing in the mirror. She wore a plain brown dress with sleeves rolled up to the elbows, but she had on high heels the color of the spring daffodil, just like the ones she brought to Mama that first time. Not even the principal at my school owned a pair of yellow shoes, and that woman was all uptown. Sister Thelma opened the Bible and began the sermon.

"Brothers and Sisters, pick up the Holy Word of Jesus and turn to the book of Gen-e-sis. To-day we're gonna talk about a man who loved God more than all others, and that man's name was Abraham. Now, God called Abraham, I said he called Abraham to make the ultimate sacrifice, to give up the life of his only son, the son he loved so dearly."

Sister Thelma pulled a large white handkerchief from her sleeve and mopped her shiny face. A little powder puff is what she needs, Mama would have whispered long ago. This night her approving eyes followed Sister Thelma around the church. Daddy snorted disagreement in his sleep. He never let Mama forget that in his humble opinion Sister Thelma had once been the worst kind of woman.

The Spoons sat right in front of us again. Their daddy tried to make the girls sit still, but he was always jumping up to pray for the sick, the sinners, or the demon possessed. Their mama, who had a bad case of the walking anemia, never said much. Sheila had her hair in a long braid and the end turned up like the crook in a cat's tail. I desperately longed to tug it gently and see what might happen. Would she turn around? There was so much I wanted to tell her. I'd say, Sheila Spoon, my mama has jumped down a rabbit hole. Used to, you only had to say her name three times to get her attention, now you had to say it six. Today she and Spencer double-crossed me and burned my jeans at the stake. Burned my blue jeans, Sheila Spoon. How could they be so hateful?

Sister Thelma grew so loud she was hard to ignore. "God said, 'Abraham' and Abraham said, 'Yes, Lord.' God said, 'Take your boy, Isaac, up to the mountain top and give him to me as an offering. Show me how much you love me,' and Abraham said, 'Yes, Lord.' Now I say to you this evenin' brothers and sisters, what would you do if God called you to give up your first-born son?"

Spencer said, "Mama?"

All five of the Spoon girls turned as one body and stared at him.

"Hah!" I laughed, a laugh that could cut glass.

Mama thumped the back of my head. The Spoons quickly faced the front. Sister Thelma wound it up.

"Abraham put the wood for the fire on Isaac's back. Abraham carried the knife and the rope. Now, Isaac wanted to know. 'Daddy,' he says, 'where is the sheep for the sacrifice?' Abraham answered, 'God will provide' and they went to the mountain top. Hallelujah!"

The holy spirit struck Sister Thelma, and she kicked off her yellow flowers and danced around the church. Hands went up and the praying began. Daddy stirred. Spencer reached over and tugged Mama's sleeve.

"What happens to the boy?" he asked.

"Hush, Spencer," said Mama, "hush and listen."

Sister Thelma calmed herself and continued. "Now when the knife was a second away from Isaac's tender breast, God said, 'Never mind, Abraham. You showed me that you love me.' And Abraham said, 'Yes, Lord.'"

And with that Sister Thelma concluded her sermon on *Great Men of the Bible.*

"But what if the knife slipped?" Spencer asked, still tugging at Mama's sleeve.

"It'll be time for the Children's Moment in a second, then you'll get to sing," she whispered.

The Bible said your old men would dream dreams and your young men would have visions, but it never said nothing about girls like me. It was clear I had to find my own way through this mess, and the time had come for action. They passed the plate, and everyone who had change put it in. Then came the Children's Moment, and Sister Thelma called for a singer for tonight's selection: *This little light of mine, I'm gonna let it shine.* Before Spencer's hand could shoot up, I was on my feet with my hand in the air and a smile that pleaded *pick me, pick me.* Sister Thelma beamed for everyone knew I had been running with the goat herd up until that moment.

"Sister Pixie and Brother Charlie's daughter, Martha, is coming up here tonight. Can I hear an A-men?"

"A-men!" said the church.

Sister Thelma strapped on her accordion.

Mama looked horrified as I scooted past her. Spencer pouted and banged his heels against the chair. Daddy kept on snoozing. I looked to see how Sheila Spoon was taking it. She leaned forward in her seat. I owned that girl's attention. Following the same path the cockroach had taken on our first night at God's House of Whole Truth, finally I was standing at the altar. I locked my knees so they wouldn't shake. Sister Thelma smiled warmly at me with her fingers poised over the accordion keys.

"You know the words?" she asked.

"Yes, ma'am."

She started playing, but I didn't sing so she stopped and the accordion gave a little squawk.

"Martha."

"Yes, ma'am?" I was sweating now, my body growing hot. I could feel sticky puddles under my arms. It didn't matter though.

"Anytime you're ready."

The church giggled.

They had all asked for it, so I took a deep breath, and let it rip.

"My ba-bee does the hank-y pank-y."

The accordion squawked again, then died.

Sister Thelma's face changed from surprise to disappointment, then it stuck on anger. Her disappointed look might have stopped me if she had stayed with it, but I was accustomed to people being mad at me.

"My ba-bee does the hank-y pank-y."

My voice was weak at first, but I patted my foot and moved my shoulders and sang it again louder, so they could hear me in Sinner's Alley. I gave it the proper face scrunch just like all of Spencer's ex-rock and roll singers.

"*My ba-bee does the hank-y pank-y.*"

I didn't know anymore words to the song and felt embarrassed about that, but the show must go on.

"*My ba-bee does the hank-y pank-y.*"

I opened my eyes and looked out into the congregation, the first time I'd seen everyone from this point of view. At first, I didn't have the courage to look at anyone but Sheila. She gave me both hairy eyebrows. Brother Spoon rubbed his temples. Sister Spoon sadly shook her head. My eyes carefully avoided the row where my own family sat.

"Does this child have a mother?" Sister Thelma said over my shoulder.

"*My ba-bee does the hank-y pank-y.*"

Someone called out, "Work it, Sweet Lips!" Whack! Whack! Whack! It was the train tunnel bum who yelled, and the old grandma was beating him with her cane. Every good cause must have a martyr. I swear the wheelchair boy was keeping time, and the sight of that lifted me to a higher plane. It was then I had the vision, or maybe this was the Holy Ghost.

Sheila Spoon and I stood on a stage with red velvet curtains. We sang into our hairbrushes and did the pony in our white go-go boots. I looked out into the audience, and Sister Thelma's Godzilla hair fell to her waist, and she shimmied like a cow shaking flies. The wheelchair boy broke his ropes and jumped free. The bum raised his hands to the sky, and all his dirt fell right off. The old grandma grabbed Brother Spoon, and they did a naughty hootchie-kootchie. All the people started dancing in their seats, dancing like people who didn't need to be saved from anything. Then the vision spread to the streets, and the unshaved man standing in the shadows was healed. From there it went all over the earth. And the last thing I knew before the vision died: everyone in the whole wide world owned a pair of white go-go boots.

Mama grabbed me then and shoved me back down the aisle, her claw on my arm, her breath hot on my neck. We passed by the Spoons, and Sheila stared at the floor. Mama pushed me into my seat. Spencer was bug-eyed. Daddy gave me his best dirty look.

"Do you think you're too old to get a whipping?" he said loud enough for the whole church to hear.

"No, Daddy." I hung my head. I didn't think about this part when I made my singing debut.

Spencer leaned over to put in his two cents' worth.

"You going to hell now for sure," he said. "Ain't she, Mama?"

Mama took her seat and stared straight ahead like nothing was happening.

"Take her outside, Charlie," she said from the side of her mouth.

"But, Mama," I whimpered. Not that, please, not that. Mama always had a hissy fit when Daddy whipped me or Spencer. She said he hit too hard, and she'd make him stop after one or two licks with the belt. She couldn't be telling him to take me outside.

"Take her outside, Charlie. Now."

My stomach curdled.

She opened up her hymnbook and put her arm around Spencer. Before I had a chance to say anything else, Daddy pushed me through the church doors, and I stumbled down the steps. I started bawling.

"Daddy, I'm sorry," I yelled, "I didn't mean to."

He dragged me down the sidewalk to our car and threw me in the back seat. He got in front and slammed the door. He took out a cigarette and blew angry smoke out the window. I sat waiting and tried to get my blubbering under control.

Watching.

Waiting.

I felt my heart slowing down.

So why wasn't he killing me?

He turned the keys in the ignition and started fiddling with the dials on the radio. Nothing on. He switched it off. He flicked his cigarette butt out the window.

The tears dried on my face.

I made myself small. I became a minor offense. A petty joke. Not worth fooling with.

Minutes passed.

He had forgotten me.

"Shut the fuck up, Martha," Daddy finally said, even though I hadn't said a word out loud. He lit another cigarette. We were still sitting there like that when church let out.

Chapter Five
Possum Tracks, 1970

That summer may have been all about free love and protest songs in some places, but not where I lived. My parents didn't discuss the dying war in Vietnam or the missing boys on the block. Instead they talked about the leak in the car's engine, and how were we going to get it fixed? Daddy moaned about his truck-driving job, and how tired he felt after unloading boxes all day, and how the honest working man could never get ahead. Mama's thoughts concerned Revelations and how the End Times was upon us. It disgusted Daddy. More and more, he grabbed his pack of Camels and headed for the door. We never knew where he went, and I was always relieved to have him out of the house.

In the old days when Daddy left, Mama wailed and went to bed for two-and-a-half hours. A dizzy spell, she'd claim afterwards. Then she washed her hair and started copying the latest bouffant from *Hairstyles of Hollywood.* Since she married Jesus, there was less wailing, fewer pin curls.

Spencer and me were expected to stay out of their way. He made a pretend church in the cool under the house and played there for hours, preaching to the worms and healing the brokenhearted spiders. Many centipedes were saved. When he tired of that, he fought the battles of the Apocalypse, all seven of them, with his armies of toy soldiers and horses. Anyone who walked by could look in and see his pale sweaty face.

"Scorpion Tail...Bezelbub...Destroyer," he whispered to the darkness.

I owned a hand-me-down mini-bike with a magnificent horn that came off an eighteen wheeler. Daddy put it on for me one day when he was mad at the neighbors. Every day during the first week of summer vacation, I rode over to Spoon's house. My bike ate up the streets that separated us, streets filled with houses that all looked the same. A-frame, with a door and two windows, a chimney jutting from the roof. One was painted white, the next was blue, and the third was yellow. Over and over again white, blue and yellow as if those were the only colors of paint on sale. For six days I rode to Sheila Spoon's block and circled her house. It was yellow just like mine. We had so much in common. She might be out in her yard, and I could say "hey." But she never was. Sometimes I saw a curtain move, and I knew those girls were inside watching me, probably giggling behind their hands.

This was the seventh day.

I rode around the house six times faster than the speed of light and on the seventh time I braked right in front of it, skidding sideways. I straddled my bike, grabbed the bulb of my horn, gave it a mighty squeeze, and shouted: "Hey, Sheila Spoon!"

The house shimmered in the heat.

What was that?

The door opened.

Who was that?

Sheila poked her head out.

Her body followed.

She walked down the steps and the sidewalk.

My heart raced around my chest like a squirrel twirling around a tree.

She walked right up to me.

She stared.

I stared back.

She raised a hairy eyebrow.

I tried to, but my eyebrow wouldn't budge.

Sheila Spoon spoke.

"I asked Daddy and he said you could come in."

"I can?" I asked, disbelieving.

"Yeah," she answered. "He said watching you is making him dizzy."

"Are you sure?"

"Yeah," she answered. "I was standing right there when he said it."

"That's not what I mean." I bit my lip. "Are you sure *you* want me to come in?"

"Yeah." She smiled.

I tooted my horn twice.

"C'mon," she said.

I carefully laid down my bike in the front yard and followed her into the house, like the moon follows the earth.

Sheila Spoon and I spent every moment we could together. She had to help more now with the cooking and cleaning since Number One, her oldest sister, had gotten married and escaped the Spoon Penitentiary. Even so, we shared the hand-me-down mini-bike, Sheila riding in the v of the handlebars with her straggle hair blowing back and me on the banana seat. She had started getting her shape, as all the women called it, but she could still fit. We pushed the bike to the top of the hill by my house and went flying down those hairpin curves all the way to the river. We darted in and out of traffic causing minor head-on collisions. We ran old people off the sidewalks and learned new curse words.

This Saturday morning, I sat on Sheila's porch talking to her through the screen door while she fried sausage. When I first started going over there, I went in and helped, but I had not grown my woman's hands yet and plates crashed in the floor, potatoes stuck to the frying pan, and little girls showed up with their dresses on backwards. Sister Spoon had said, "Thanks for your help, Martha, next time why don't you wait on the porch, and I'll fix you a glass of ice tea." Finally, after the younger Spoons were fed and watered, the jailer unlocked the door, and my best friend roamed free for a few hours.

We planned a big adventure. Today we were sneaking over to the House in the Alley. If you said it that way, like it was capitalized, your listener understood exactly which house you meant. No one knew who owned it, but older kids came and went at all hours. At first sight, it was just a little place in the alley behind the Piggly Wiggly store, but look again. In a neighborhood where a six pack of Schlitz was considered high living, empty wine bottles waited by the trash can. A funny smell surrounded the house. Some claimed a gas leak because a walk down the alley could make a grown man dizzy. Three angry young rednecks who wore grease in their hair and stowed Arkansas toothpicks in their boots declared they were going to clean the place up. They were seen entering the house one Saturday night. Three days later they stumbled out, meek as new kittens, and flashed peace signs to the cops cruising by. A neighbor swore that one wore a garland of dandelions in his hair, but no one believed that. The most damning evidence? A wrecked Volkswagen Beetle parked there with California license plates. Grown-ups alleged the whole state of California was just one big den of iniquity. If one of theirs had settled here, it was like a rat bringing rabies. The young people who lived in the house in the alley had probably committed unimaginable sins. Me and the Spoon couldn't wait to find out.

Now all we had to do was get there. Our plan was to go a roundabout way just in case anyone was tailing us. It was my turn to pedal first, and Spoon jumped on the handlebars. After Mama burned my jeans, I learned how to tuck my dress between my legs so my possum wouldn't show. The first time I called down there "my possum," the Spoon had given me the eyebrow. Well, I had explained, Mama always says *possible* or *possum* and that's all I know.

"Uh, Martha," she said, "a possum is a little animal with pink ears and a tail like a rat."

"What's it really called?" I challenged her. Neither of us knew. It turned out that the female voice of authority at the Spoon's house always said, "don't forget to wash where the Indian threw the hatchet." When she told me that, we laughed so hard we had to mop ourselves up off the floor.

We pedaled by the Piggly Wiggly first and didn't even look down the alley toward you-know-what. A few blocks away, we saw my grandma and Spencer coming from the store. They were holding hands, and it looked like an old woman leading a little boy. I knew it was probably the other way around. She had come to live with us that summer, and she was pretty messed up. It had all started when mystery packages arrived from her house in the country. Spencer got the good knife and half an onion. I got some old carrots that had wilted in the sun. Mama got a book of matches and a pinch of salt. Daddy got three cherry tomatoes.

"Well," Mama had said nervously, "we can make some soup."

Worried calls to the country were made on the neighbor man's telephone. Some second cousins were dispatched to check on her. Their report was not good. They had to sell the cows and everything else and pack her up. She had to leave that old house where every feather mattress had been the birthplace or the death bed of someone she loved.

"It is necessary," Mama explained, "she is old and sick."

"She gets a check, doesn't she?" Daddy asked.

"What difference does that make?" Mama said, "She's my mother."

"What difference does it make? Have you seen the light bill this month?"

I looked forward to her arrival. The day we met the Greyhound she didn't show up. The next weekend Daddy put a quart of oil in the car engine and a case in the trunk, and he and Mama drove off in a cloud of smoke. The woman they brought back was not the same one I'd left behind. This woman was thin and dirty and snuff stained her chin. She still had her overalls, though, and man-sized rubber boots floppy on her feet.

"Hi, Grandma," I said to her at the curb, and she just stared.

"Little Pixie," she finally said and we hugged. I could feel her bones.

"No," I said, "it's me, Martha."

Her hug didn't change.

"Martha," she said. "I've missed my helper."

"I'm not so little anymore." My grandma shrank, and I grew taller.

She spied Spencer. "There's me a boy, too," she said, and we made it a three-way hug.

He moved to the living room couch, and Grandma slept with me on my old iron bed in the back room. Her suitcases and boxes and bags took it over, and we could barely walk around. Every three a.m. she woke and wandered through the house, talking to herself.

"Where is the hoe for the strawberries? Where is the yellow rose that grows beside my kitchen door? Where is my Crazy Quilt?"

"On your bed," Mama's weary voice came out of the night, "go lay in it."

Spencer and me tried to help, we really did, so early one morning we went out back and started digging her a garden, even though the neighbors had all ready started picking tomatoes and giving them away.

Grandma came out of the house and watched, one strap of her overalls unhitched, her face suspicious, like we were doing something she'd never seen done before. It wasn't long though before she had rummaged through the trash and found a can to hold bait. She squatted down in the freshly turned dirt and plucked white cutworms. I didn't have the heart to tell her the only place to fish was the muddy Arkansas, and all it had to offer was toothy alligator gar and poison catfish. You might catch a big fat turd.

Spencer picked up a worm and dropped it in her can.

"That's a big one, Boy," she said, squinting up at him. She could never remember his name.

"Yes, ma'm." He grinned as if she'd called him prince. He looked at me. "I probably remind her of that fast kid in the Tarzan movies."

Then the little dope pounded his chest and swung off on pretend vines.

Grandma made a little circle in the air by her temple, the loco sign.

"That's right, Grandma," I said, as Spencer swung from vine to vine. "He's crazy."

"Crazy," she said. "That boy is crazy, Pixie."

I started to tell her that I was Martha, but before I could, a scream erupted from the house. A window was thrown open by unseen hands, and smoke poured out.

"I made a fire in the wood stove," said Grandma, "must have forgot to open the damper."

Daddy cussed loud enough for the neighbors to hear, then he and Mama came running out of the back door, coughing with tears running down their faces.

"We don't have a wood stove, Grandma. It uses gas."

"Oh," she said and went back to rummaging in the dirt.

Still it was better to have half a grandma, than no grandma at all. And, when the electric fan blew cool air across our bed at night and the white sheets waltzed in the moonlight, I touched her leg with my toe and could not tell she had changed at all.

"Hold on!" I yelled and skidded the brakes on the bike. We turned around in the middle of the street to avoid Grandma and Spencer. No witnesses. Soon we were flying down the hill to the river. The sun shone brightly that day, and the empty buildings we sailed by looked less lonely. In the flood of '64, water had risen this high and washed out the shops where flowers were sold, where the dentist pulled teeth, where a barber had given haircuts to three generations. The broken windows of the All Night Cafe glittered in the crystal sunlight. Every kid in town had sat on a round stool at the counter, drunk hot milk coffee, and eaten sugar doughnuts. Going there was a reward for good behavior and a cure for just about everything else.

"They had the best!" I shouted at Spoon and pointed to the cafe. She shook her head and the wind carried her words back to me.

"We weren't allowed to go there!"

Could have been the money because they never had any extra. Could have been that something about the cafe offended Brother Spoon. He walked tight with the Lord, and it had made him peculiar.

Sheila Spoon's loss caused me to feel a wave of sadness, but it didn't linger on such a pretty day. We were coasting down the hill, but it was time to pump. I could not give her hot milk coffee and sugar doughnuts at the All Night Cafe. I could not give her normal parents. But I could race this bike and give her the ride of a lifetime. My legs were strong; my heart wide open. My dress flew up, and I didn't care. Soon Spoon's hair whipped me in the face, and she rewarded me with one long scream of joy. Sadness couldn't catch us now. An old timer was crossing the street at the bottom of the hill. When he looked up and saw our magnificence bearing down on him, he didn't bother to run; I swear he just stroked right on the spot.

The Spoon and I rested on the riverbank and talked about our future. She had never seen the ocean, either, and thought Galveston was a grand idea. We'd leave as soon as our high school graduation was over. She added her dream to mine, playing the electric guitar in an all-girl rock and roll band. I had never heard of such a thing. Spoon was about to invent a new art form. She'd had a minor drawback, though, since her parents wouldn't allow her to own a musical instrument. When the Spoon complained to her mama, she was pointed in the direction of the family's tambourine. Sister Spoon had dusted her hands and walked out of the room as if the problem were solved. An hour later, when her mama heard a lot of racket and it wasn't *Jesus on the Mainline*, she came back in. The little girls were singing back-up, and Sheila was shaking out *House of the Rising Sun.* Her mama didn't tell on her, but now the tambourine was off-limits, too. We would get her a guitar at the first pawn shop we came to on the way to Galveston. Two dollars and seventy-three cents was already buried under the house in a mason jar for this very purpose. We had earned the money collecting coke bottles and selling them for the refund. Sometimes the neighbor man would call us over to his house and pay a quarter to whoever found his teeth.

"Look," she pointed at a maple leaf floating downstream. "A starfish."

It was her turn to pedal, and I perched on the handlebars. When we got to the bottom of the hill, I figured a crowd would be huddled around the stroke victim. No one was there. I guessed they'd already hauled the old timer's cadaver to the morgue. Spoon pushed the bike up the hill to the city pool, the last stop before the House in the Alley. We threw the bike down in the parking lot and went over to the fence. It had turned awful hot, and we held on to the metal wire and looked in with longing. It cost fifty cents to get in. Even if we had it, we'd have to wear bathing suits, and we weren't allowed to show that much skin.

"I wish…" said Spoon.

"Me, too." I answered.

"Just this once," she said.

"No, all the time."

Bold Diane Bickerstaff Buck sunned on the side of the pool in a red polka dotted bikini. Her tan was perfect.

"What would you give to be Diane for a day?" I asked the Spoon.

Spoon made a gagging noise. "I hate her. She's never passed up a chance to be ugly to me."

A high school boy picked up Diane and threatened to drop her into the water. She squealed like a happy little pig. Everyone watched. Then the boy did toss her in, and she came up laughing with nary an eyelash out of place.

"But what would you give to be Diane for a day?" I persisted.

This time Spoon gave me the hairy eyebrow. She wore a long sleeved shirt. A skirt that came down past her knees. A pair of hand-me-down tennis shoes. No strings in the shoes.

"Four sisters," she finally answered.

That cracked us up. We made faces at the pool kids, so when they looked up, they saw us clowning. For a moment, they were the ones in the cage, and we were the ones free.

Closing in on our final destination, we carefully checked the streets for spies. The plan was to walk down the alley calling for our pretend lost cat. If anybody wanted to know, her name was Miss Kitty and her fur was strawberry blonde. She had been missing for three days, and this was the only place left where we had not called her name. We'd leave the bike in the ditch, walk up and down the alley twice, then go up to the front door of the House and knock. Maybe they'd invite us in. If not, we'd still get a good look.

On the right were people's backyards. On the left, the same. I sniffed the air. Spoon did, too. So far nothing different. We passed a sycamore tree and spiky pom poms littered the ground. A few more steps and the back fence of the Piggly Wiggly rose at our left. The smell of their dumpster washed over us, overflowing with rotten food. I stopped and looked, wanting to investigate its bounty, but Spoon said, *not now, Martha.* Then she gasped and grabbed my arm.

"What?"

"We forgot to call the cat!"

Immediately we began whispering, "Kitty, kitty, kitty, Miss Kitty, Miss Kitty."

The house was in sight. Black paint covered the windows, so no one could see in. Big green wine bottles filled the trashcan. The crushed Volkswagen Beetle with the California license plates still slept there. A strange big-winged bird perched on the fence across from the house. It had a neck like a question mark. When we came close, it took off with a flutter of wings and began to fly in a circle above the house.

"Is that a buzzard?" I asked, but before Spoon could answer, a van came over the rise in the alley and screeched to a stop. There was no place to hide.

It was old and painted rainbow colors, and all kinds of people hung out of the windows. A gypsy caravan, I decided. The music pouring from their stereo was loud and deep. The side door opened, and a woman, no, a man, hopped out. He had curly red hair that came down his back, big legged blue jeans that dragged the ground, a guitar case slung over his shoulder. His friends jumped out, too. None of the girls wore bras, and they were bouncing all over the place. Mama would have made a face like someone was holding a sack of fresh shit under her nose.

Then the red headed man noticed us.

"Look," he said to his friends. "Jailbait."

They glanced at us, laughed, and streamed into the house. Red took his guitar case off and left it on the porch. He took a few steps toward us. We took a few steps back. He squatted down in the alley and stared.

"What's happenin'?" He asked. Someone had knocked out his two front teeth. He had some straggle hair on his chin and lots of freckles. His eyebrows were paler than the rest of him, and they sat on his forehead like furry caterpillars. He sure was ugly.

"We're looking for Miss Kitty." I started to say more, but Spoon jabbed me with her elbow.

Red stroked his chin. He looked from Spoon to me, then back to Spoon. His eyes went from the bottom of her feet to the top of her head and down again, taking inventory of everything she owned.

"Well," I said, "I think I hear Mama calling." I grabbed Spoon's arm and started tugging. She wouldn't budge.

Red pulled the hair on his chin. His caterpillar eyebrows humped the hill of his forehead. "Either of you girls ever had your pussy ate?"

That confused me. At first, I thought he was talking about Miss Kitty. Then I realized he meant something else, and I saw him with a knife and fork, white napkin tied around his neck. Me on a plate.

I looked at Spoon. She looked at me. We started backing up. Then we turned at the exact same time and ran so hard our shadows couldn't keep up. The red headed man laughed and laughed, and the laugh chased us all the way back to where we had hidden the bike. We had to leave our shadows behind, we couldn't go back and get them, and I was sure they sat down on the ground and cried like babies.

The big winged bird still circled the sky. Spoon kept running. I jerked the bike from the ditch and got on.

Finally, I caught up with her. She was panting, all white around the gills. I got off the bike and pushed it, and we walked like that for five and a half blocks.

"Forget about that creep. Get on the handlebars," I told her. "We'll go down the hill again.

"No." She threw her hair over her shoulder and turned toward home. "I'm getting too big to fit there."

Chapter Six

The Beautiful River, 1970

Way above the sewer pipe on the Arkansas River where the knobby kneed cypress grew, there was a little sandy cove. Spanish moss hung from the trees, and raccoons traded mussel shells on the bank. The humid air was as thick as the meringue on a buttermilk pie. I had been there three times this month right around the time dusk slid into night, the spot where the people of God's House of Whole Truth held their baptizings. This evening it was Mama and Spencer's turn. Not me. No sir. I wasn't dipping a toe in. Daddy said I didn't have to. For once, he was on my side.

"Water moccasins," I whispered in Spencer's ear. "Cottonmouths."

He told on me, of course. Mama assured him that snakes avoided people, and even if one slithered close, Spencer would not be harmed because he was washed in the Blood of the Lamb.

After she left the room, I had more to say.

"Did you hear what happened to Sweet Pea?"

Spencer's ears perked up. All the neighborhood kids loved that dog, but no one loved her more than him. She didn't allow anyone but Spencer to care for her. He'd get Mama's eyebrow tweezers and go over her as carefully as a surgeon, dropping ticks one by one in a can of alcohol.

Good dog, good dog, he'd say, as each bloodsucker drowned in its bath. Sweet Pea disappeared early in the summer, and Spencer had walked the streets for hours calling her name.

"Some kids found her on the riverbank last week. What was left of her that is. Two long teeth and a piece of tail. Everybody says one of them giant snakes got her."

Spencer wasn't buying.

"How'd they know it was Sweet Pea?"

"Someone or *something* had left her rabies tag hanging from a tree limb, dummy."

He got it that time and ran hiccupping to Mama again. I loved teasing him. It was so easy.

Grandma and me were in the back room where we slept. It was so crowded there was barely a trail between the creaky old iron bed and the dresser. I stood in front of the mirror brushing my hair while Grandma sat on the bed. Sometimes she talked to people who weren't there, but this day she was mostly quiet and watchful. It was my job to get her dressed. She wanted to wear her overalls and rubber boots, but Mama had stomped into the room and pulled out Grandma's purple dress with the green collar, the one that made her look like a skinny eggplant.

Changes to my body arrived daily, like the morning paper. Nobody seemed as excited as me. My headline announcements about new bumps and lumps were met with blank stares. I was sprouting everywhere, and I could barely button my dress. If Mama didn't buy me some new clothes soon, I was going to bust out and cause a disgrace. Couldn't she see that I was just two minutes away from becoming a woman? I had contacted the Kotex company. Now hidden away behind a dresser drawer was my starter kit: belt, booklet and white cotton pads. Spoon was lucky; she had older sisters who gave her the facts. Mama would have let me bleed to death. She wouldn't talk about anything that happened below the neck. I had long given up getting any good information from her and had to rely on the Spoon sisters, or the kids playing in the alley for all I needed to know.

"Well, that's done." I put the brush down. My hair was growing out, but that was okay since all the girls were going in for this now. But the hated long dress still marked me.

Grandma heaved herself up then so slowly and carefully, the bed and her bones made a creaking clanging noise. The sound sent my thoughts flying, and I saw a knight in rusty armor fighting to rise from a cold ground, the warm breath of his worried horse snorting over him, the tower of his enemies' castle in the near distance.

Grandma hobbled over to where I stood.

"Who is that old woman?" She was looking at herself in the mirror.

I put my arms around her and held her, and it was like holding a birdcage with a canary fluttering inside. I didn't know what else to do or what to say. The facts stared back at us. Grandma took a deep breath, then shrunk a little more.

"Now where are we going again?" she asked.

"To the river. Your daughter Pixie is getting baptized."

"I'll get my fishing pole." She moved away from my arms.

It was propped in the corner of our room.

Mama came in then and said she was ready, if I could tear myself away from that mirror. She was one to talk since she was married to the mirror before Jesus got a hold of her.

The summer sun was going down, but Daddy still sat at the kitchen table, sulking and smoking, and wouldn't get dressed until Mama pleaded. He said this was taking things a little too far and all his people were Freewill Baptists and a sprinkle on the head had always been good enough for them and just who did Pixie think she was to want something different? Then when Grandma tried to put her fishing pole in the car, it was Mama's turn to fuss. Daddy said it wouldn't hurt nothing for somebody to get a little pleasure out of the evening. Grandma got to take the pole, a can of cutworms, and her tackle box. Even with all that stuff and us in the back seat, there was still room enough for me to act out my latest show for Spencer. It was called *Run, Sweet Pea, Run.*

Sheila Spoon met us in the little park above the cove.

"I brought my camera, Sister Pixie, would you like me to take y'all's picture?"

She had a Kodak, the kind you held at your waist and looked down through the viewfinder. Everybody said Sheila had a good eye meaning the people in her pictures never had light poles growing out of their heads. Mama was so pleased. She lined us up, and Sheila snapped a few.

Daddy slouched at one end of the row, mumbling under his breath and rolling his eyes, his contempt-o-meter flying way past disdain. Mama was right next to him in a print dress, her hair, finally, a bowling ball. One hand laid gently on Daddy's arm and that was the only thing holding him in place. Grandma stood at the other end of the row in her purple outfit holding on to her fishing pole and tackle box. She didn't look fragile or confused in that moment, just waiting for us to be done with the nonsense so she could go get her a mess of fish. Then Spencer: hair combed back with Vitalis instead of the more popular Dry look, big front teeth like a beaver from all that thumb sucking. He looked like a regular goofy kid, not a boy whose Mama read to him every night from Fox's *Book of Martyrs*. Last, there was me. I put my hands on my hips and gave the camera my Marilyn Monroe sexpot look.

After the picture taking, we fell in line behind Spoon and walked through pockets of cold air down the path. Toads taxied from the weeds to the water for their nightly swim. Spencer forgot his reptile fears for a minute and started hopping after them, until Mama reminded him that he couldn't very well make a public announcement renouncing sin with frogs in his pockets. I wondered why not. Voices rose in the still air: *Shall we gather at the river/ the beautiful/ the beautiful river?*

"They're biting." Grandma moved away from all the people. She had a hook in the water before you could say *amen.*

Most of the church had showed up that evening. Miracles were known to happen at a baptizing. A woman all set for a breech birth had felt the baby flip merely by standing in the wake. Brother Spoon witnessed that his bad back was made straight. Sister Spoon testified (in a much quieter voice) that yes, indeed, she always felt stronger after a baptism just like she'd had a dose of the sassafras spring tonic. They even put the wheelchair boy in the Living Waters once. Someone pulled him out before he drowned, but his mother declared that for a day or two afterwards he had a certain glow. Sister Thelma, who was already out in the water with her dress floating around her like a lily pad, preached that when Jesus was dunked, the heavens opened up, and the Holy Ghost in the shape of a white dove flew down and sat on his shoulder, and God himself spoke: "I'm mighty pleased with you, boy."

Spoon and I stood at the edge of the crowd. She was so close I could smell her Jergen's lotion, the only beauty product the Spoon girls were allowed to use. Her long brown hair was pulled back smooth and held with a barrette, but her bangs were long and hung in her eyes. She smiled at me, and our fingers touched.

Then Sister Thelma called my mama's name, and she took off her sandals and slid down the bank and walked into the muddy water. She reached for Sister Thelma, and they held hands. Mama finally had a tight friend, too, just like me.

Daddy lit a Camel and collected some stares from the Holy Rollers, but no one had the guts to say anything to him. He just looked around, bored. Everyone grew quiet and waited.

"Now see here," Sister Thelma said in her strong voice, and even the people fishing looked up. "Sister Pixie has come this evening to be baptized in the Living Waters."

Mama smiled like a shy bride, but nodded proudly. Her ball of hair wobbled on her head. She seemed to have forgotten Daddy standing on the riverbank frowning at her. He had always been her number one, but now Jesus had taken over. I don't think Daddy knew it yet.

Sister Thelma continued.

"To be baptized is to say that you turn your back on sin. To be baptized is to say that you belong to Je-sus first and the world no more! Isn't that right, Sister Pixie?"

Mama said, "That's right."

The people said, *amen.* The people fishing said, *amen.* Dusk slid into evening time. A choir of frogs sang bass. A swarm of vampire mosquitoes settled right on us, and everyone started slapping. Down river I heard Grandma say, "I think I got one." Spencer looked like he wanted to go see, but maybe his feet grew roots and held him in place. Sister Thelma wrapped one arm around my mama's waist and put a hand on her forehead.

"I baptize you in the name of the Father, the Son, and the Holy Ghost."

She eased my mama backwards into the muddy water until she was gone from our sight. I held my breath with Mama - one, two, three - then Sister Thelma pulled her up. I saw a white dove swoop down, but it turned out to be a river gull diving for a bug. I looked around for a sign, but there was nothing. Just two wet grownups standing in the river and others watching. Then Mama raised her hands to the darkening sky.

"Shon-da-la-la-la-la."

The Holy Ghost had lit. Mama was speaking in tongues. The people shouted and praise went out. She came out of the river and did the Holy Roller shuffle as soon as she was on dry land. Everybody made room for her to dance.

"Oh, brother," said Daddy, looking both astonished and disgusted. He threw his cigarette down and stalked off.

She swooned in the spirit, and the people caught her before she hit the ground. Sister Spoon laid a large white handkerchief over Mama's knees to keep her modest.

Mama missed Spencer's baptizing. I was the only one in the family who saw it.

"Come on in, Spencer," cooed Sister Thelma, "the water's fine."

Everybody laughed. Spencer went slipping and sliding down the muddy bank to the dark water. He stopped there and looked out at Sister Thelma. She gave him an encouraging smile. He turned back and looked around at all of us, his face afraid and uncertain. He was looking for his mama, I knew, and she was passed out on the ground. Daddy was nowhere around; Grandma was fishing. Spencer's big eyes skipped right over me like I was a stranger. I felt a little sorry then that I had teased him about Sweet Pea and the snakes. It was a mean thing to do. He had become such a little brownnoser that I had almost forgotten about the real live Spencer. Together we might have been a team, but he took Mama's side and helped her burn my jeans. He became one of them and left me all alone in the family.

Even so, I didn't really want him to go into that scary water. We couldn't see what was waiting just below the ripples. There might be snakes or something worse. I skipped down the bank toward him, leaving the Spoon behind. I didn't know what I was going to say or do, maybe grab his hand and run like hell, maybe Daddy, maybe Daddy could, no, never mind. Then the people said, "Go ahead, Spencer" before I could reach him, and he stepped into the murk. Sister Thelma guided him out to where the river was waist deep. I stopped when the hem of my dress got wet. From there I watched for shadows in the water. Spencer's feet came up, and if she hadn't been holding on to his wrist, he might have floated away. I wanted to yell, hurry up, can't you see he's scared? Around here though, grown-ups did not look into the faces of children to see what they were feeling. Of course, Sister Thelma had to jazz it up because Spencer was the youngest child from Whole Truth who had ever been baptized willingly. Then the dark sky met the dark water, and all I could see of Spencer was his white shirt.

Lightening bugs blinked off and on, and the people followed them up the hill to their parked cars. I tried to go to Spencer when he came out of the river, but Mama, revived by then, beat me to it. He was wet and shivery even though the night was warm and muggy. I gathered up Grandma and her catch of three little catfish and her tackle box and cane fishing pole.

The people shook Mama's hand and congratulated her on receiving the gift of tongues.

"I didn't think He would give it to me," she kept saying as we worked our way through the crowd of well wishers. "I didn't think I was worthy." She cried and laughed at the same time, like a beauty queen who had just won the crown. Sister Spoon pulled a handkerchief from her sleeve and gently wiped the tears from Mama's face.

Daddy paced back and forth by the car, so we hurried on over with the crowd trailing behind us.

Daddy stopped in his tracks. "That was quite a display you put on this evenin', Pixie." He said it loud enough for everyone to hear.

Mama bit the smile off her face.

"Get in the car," he said.

Spencer and Grandma and me crawled in the back seat. Daddy got behind the wheel.

Mama reached for the door handle.

"Wait. You're dripping wet." Daddy made a big show of spreading out some old rags on his upholstery.

"Now, you can get in."

Mama reached for the door handle. Paused. She turned to the crowd. "Good night," she called shyly.

"Good night, Sister Pixie, good night." They waved.

She smiled and reached for the door handle again.

Daddy floored the gas.

We shot forward. He slammed on the brake. Our heads hit the back of the front seat.

The car purred like a big cat.

"Get in the car, Pixie," Daddy called over his shoulder.

Mama walked to where we were.

The crowd stared at the ground.

"Oh no," someone whispered.

Mama reached for the door handle.

Daddy punched it.

We were flung back.

Daddy stomped the brake.

We didn't hit our heads this time.

"What is happening?" cried Grandma.

Spencer touched his forehead. "I think I have a fever." He shivered.

I felt pukeous.

Mama walked up to the car.

"Charlie, please," she begged. "Let me in."

"Get in," he said. "I ain't stopping you."

She touched the handle.

He punched it.

He slammed it.

We jerked.

"Don't do this, Charlie," Mama called out.

I couldn't see the crowd any longer. We had lurched all the way to the end of the parking lot.

"I don't understand what is happening," Grandma cried.

"It's ok, Grandma." Spencer patted her knee. "Daddy's playing a game."

"It's not a game," I muttered, curling up in the floorboard and wrapping my arms around my head.

Daddy made a u-turn and pulled up alongside Mama.

"Why don't you get in, Pixie? Why you standing out there in the parking lot?"

This time I heard the car door open and close.

Spencer spoke up in a still small voice.

"One of my shoes came off in the water."

Daddy slammed his fist against the steering wheel.

"Who allowed that child to go in the river in his shoes? You think I got the money to buy another pair? Do you? Do you?"

Mama made a strangled noise in her throat. Doomed. No matter what she said. She whispered something we couldn't hear.

"What did you say?" Daddy gunned the gas pedal, and the car backfired.

Mama spoke a little louder but still a whisper.

"Je-sus Je-sus Je-sus Je-sus."

"I've had it up to here with Jesus, Pixie. I think you need to call my name once in awhile. How 'bout that?"

And Mama whispered, "Je-sus Je-sus Je-sus Je-sus."

"Any woman who'd make a display of herself like that…."

"Je-sus Je-sus Je-sus Je-sus."

"I said I've had enough."

"Je-sus Je-sus Je-sus Je-sus."

"Make a choice, Pixie."

"Je-sus Je-sus Je-sus Je-sus." She pulled away from him.

It went like that until we got home. Daddy slammed to a stop in front of the house, and we all scrambled out: Grandma, with her little mess of white meat and whiskers, Spencer, one shoe on and one shoe gone, Mama, all the beauty of her victory wiped out. Daddy peeled out again, but the smoking car jerked and died and sparks shot from the tailpipe. He cursed so loud, the dogs in the next block woke up, and their howling ran all the way up the hill.

Chapter Seven

Chocolate Covered Cherries, 1970

After the night of Mama's baptism in the Living Waters, Daddy disappeared. Buzzing about it went on night and day. Spencer thought he had gone on a run in his truck to Los Angeles, California. I thought he shacked up with a secret family, probably a red head who owned three or four knee biters. Grandma said, "*Charlie who?*" Brother Spoon even went down to the dock where Daddy's truck was loaded early every morning, but the workers always said he'd just left. One minute, Mama sat with her eyes closed and a cold rag on her forehead; the next minute she'd be throwing pans across the kitchen. She'd say, *what if he is not home by the first? I'm ten dollars short on the rent.* The next minute she'd get her backbone up and say, *that sorry excuse of a husband better not show his face round here again.* Sister Spoon dropped in twice with a pot of collards. She ate them every day for her anemia and claimed they'd put color back into Mama's cheeks. I couldn't say that the collards had improved Sister Spoon's looks any.

Sister Thelma came by often, and the women sat with a box of tissue at the kitchen table. She offered Mama a job in her housecleaning business, and Mama thought she might have to take it. She was nervous, though, since she had never had a job before or cleaned any house except her own. There was also the question of who would watch Grandma since she couldn't be left alone. They went back and forth about what should be done and listening to them made me dizzy and sick to my stomach. Anytime they started yapping, I left the room and sat under the house if Spencer wasn't already there.

Toward the end of the month, Sister Thelma handed Mama a little envelope of cash, a special collection taken at the church. It really touched Mama's heart since the people at God's House of Whole Truth were so poor they couldn't afford fatback for the beans.

Meanwhile middle school started, and there was no money for new clothes or school supplies. People made fun of my Pentecostal dresses like I knew they would, so I stopped talking in class and practiced becoming invisible. No more shows. I moved quietly as possible and learned to walk without leaving footprints, just like an Indian. I stuck close to Spoon and tried on her tough girl attitude when I did attract attention.

Late one autumn afternoon when Daddy had been gone for three weeks, the rest of the family sat around the kitchen table. The last of the day's sunlight streamed through the window and tried hard to make the room look pretty. A pot of pinto beans simmered on the back of the stove, and the smell told our bellies *soon*. The icebox hummed its usual song. Despite Daddy's disappearance, nothing had really changed that much yet, so at that moment we were pretending he was at work or over at the neighbor's or down at the Dairy DeLite throwing our money away on the pinball machine.

With scissors and paper, I made an I.D. bracelet for Grandma because she couldn't hold on to our address anymore. She'd gotten lost for hours the day before, and the neighbor man found her wandering around the Piggly Wiggly parking lot.

"Here," I said, "let me put this on your wrist."

She held out her arm, and it was like the stick Hansel and Gretel had used to fool the witch who wanted to eat them.

Mama had given her the job of cleaning the beans for tomorrow. There was a big pile in front of her, and she went through them one by one, picking out the dirt and pebbles. In between beans, she teased Spencer about all his girlfriends. He went along with it even though all I had ever seen him do with girls was put spiders in their braids and laugh when they screamed. He worked on his multiplication tables with Mama and couldn't seem to get past six times seven. He sat with his elbows on the table and a look of fierce concentration on his face.

Then the icebox cut out, and we all looked up.

"It'll start again," said Mama, and we waited.

My mama and daddy bought the icebox at a pawnshop the day after they were married, so it was dented and rusty even then. It labored in the summertime, and the milk soured. In the winter, the freezer compartment froze over. Many times Daddy had got down on his belly and gone into the motor with a screwdriver. He said it hung together with electrical tape and chicken wire, and we should never sneeze when we were standing nearby.

The icebox didn't start again, and we waited.

Mama looked around the table at us. She smiled, and there was no fear in it. I did not know how. We couldn't fix the icebox ourselves, and a repairman cost money. Grandma's social security check had already been spent this month. The last of our food was in there. Mama could stay calm, but I put the scissors and paper down.

"Mama, do you want me to get the frozen stuff out and take it over to the neighbor man?"

"No," she said. "Six times seven, Spencer."

"Sixty-five," he answered.

"Shore wish we had my old icebox," said Grandma. "It was a dandy." She pushed one more bean into the good pile.

"While I'm over there, I could ask him to come take a look at it."

Mama shook her head.

"Well, do you want me to go get the hammer? I know where Daddy hits the motor."

Another shake of the head from Mama.

Something snapped, crackled, and popped inside the icebox, and it wasn't Rice Crispies. A little pool of water formed in the floor. I thought about our groceries melting.

"Mama, don't we have hamburger meat in the freezer?"

She was looking at Spencer. "How did you get sixty-five out of six times seven?"

Spencer sighed and put his head on the table. She rubbed his shoulders like he was a prizefighter facing a difficult round. Then she turned her attention to me.

"Martha, we do have hamburger in the freezer and some vegetable soup that Sister Spoon made special for us and three sausage patties and a piece of salt pork that will season them beans cooking on the back of the stove. I know exactly what is in my icebox and my cupboards, too, just as I have every day since long before you were even a thought in my mind. Now will you leave it alone? I told you it would start again."

Crazy woman crazy woman crazy woman crazy woman. We were going to die of starvation. I could see it now. The Spoon would miss me at school. At first, she'd think I was sick. She'd come knocking on the door, and we'd all be too weak to answer. Finally, she'd hear something. It'd be me whispering her name with my last dying breath. She'd break down the door and save our lives. Mama'd be arrested for endangering the welfare of one elder and two innocents. Spoon's family would adopt me. At that point, my story crumbled as I could not imagine living in the same house with the mad dog Brother Spoon and his pale snail wife.

The icebox didn't start again, and we waited.

Grandma pushed a dented bean into the bad pile.

I sat closest to the icebox, and now the puddle of water lapped at my chair. It reminded me of something I'd seen on the "Late Late Show." I started going into this Steve McQueen Blob thing, you know, the show where the Blob from outer space lands and chases all the teenagers into a diner, and no grownup will believe there is a Blob because after all it was just kids telling the story? Any second now the cold slime would wrap around my leg, and a quick jerk would pull me under the table. Grandma would continue counting beans. Mama would just sit there. Spencer might look.

This time he had the answer.

"Mama, why don't we pray?"

"I am praying," she answered. "I never stop."

"Let's pray like they do in church when someone is sick. Like this." He rose from his chair and walked over to the dead icebox and laid his hands on it. He had the same bulldog look on his face that he wore for math. Man, that kid was a fool.

Mama nodded and rose from her chair.

There went another one.

She walked carefully around the growing pool of water and placed her hands on the icebox.

Grandma looked from the beans to them, then at me.

I shrugged.

"Y'all care to join us?" Mama asked.

We both shook our heads.

Mama spread her fingers wide and leaned close to the icebox. "Lord, we are your faithful servants...."

The afternoon gave up the ghost, and Spencer pulled the string and turned the light on. Mama made me mop the floor since I was the faithless one. The icebox had trembled and shook and started again just like she had said. I didn't believe for a second that the spirit had flashed down from heaven and healed it. I could see God and old man Moses sitting on a fluffy white cloud. Moses was wearing a gray felt hat, and he had an ear horn. God had said, "Somebody's calling my name." Moses had said, "What was that?" And God looked all around the heavens and pinpointed this universe, this solar system, this planet, this country, this state, this city, this block, this house, this kitchen. God rose from his easy chair, hitched up his pants, and said, "Got a little hardware problem." He had pointed his finger right at our icebox and zapped it. Old man Moses had said, "Did I ever tell you about the time..." God answered patiently, "I was there, Moses, I was there."

Right.

Now Mama and them were smacking their lips over the pinto beans like it was some kind of party. She poured ice tea in our glasses while Spencer slurped milk and gave himself a moustache. Grandma buttered the cornbread.

"Missy," Grandma said, "put that mop down and come get you a bowl 'fore they get cold."

Mama and Spencer were so happy over their little miracle. Grandma was happy they were happy. I wasn't happy, but then I thought about what a good story it would be when I told it to Spoon at school the next day. She would shake her head sadly. She might even reach for a piece of my hair and move it out of my eyes. She'd probably tell me about the time her very own daddy had prayed for their transmission. We'd turn from where we stood and walk off together hand in hand into the sunset. After I thought about that for awhile, I was o.k. enough to accept another piece of cornbread.

When the last bean was served with the spoon and there was nothing but crumbs in the pan, a car door slammed. Heavy boots fell on the step. Grandma pulled her sweater tight, and Spencer wiped the smile off his face. The kitchen window frosted over. We became ice statues in a snow palace. Mama's eyes closed; her lips moved. She was calling Jesus on the mainline. I hoped she didn't get a busy signal because the footsteps coming across the living room floor sounded like crackling ice in a frozen wasteland.

Daddy surprised us, though, by walking quietly into the kitchen with a box of chocolate-covered cherries and placing them on the table in front of Mama. He wore his work uniform with his name stitched in cursive letters over the front pocket. He pulled up the extra chair, swung it around, straddled it. Daddy's face was peaked as if he had been sick or not getting enough sleep. He did not look like he was in an ass-kicking mood. My fear thawed and my heart beat and my blue fingers tingled.

Grandma leaned toward me and whispered.

"Who is that man?"

"That's Charlie, your son-in-law."

"How y'all been doing?" Daddy asked. He fished in his shirt pocket for the pack of Camels. The fire from his lighter warmed the air.

Mama said, "Fine." She used to twirl her hair when she was nervous, but tonight it was all done up with not an extra piece hanging down. She folded her hands in her lap and stared at the wall over Grandma's head.

Daddy looked at Spencer and me.

"How you kids been doing?"

Spencer said, "Fine."

I said, "Fine."

Grandma knew her line.

She said, "Fine."

"Sounds like everybody is fine," Daddy concluded. He looked around the room. "How come this floor is so wet in here? What happened?"

"The icebox cut out tonight. Spencer and me laid hands, and Lord Jesus saw fit to fix it for us." Mama still wasn't looking at him.

Now this kind of remark usually made Daddy snort, but tonight he nodded as if Jesus the Repairman was a regular visitor to our house.

"Do you remember when we bought that icebox, Pixie? At Maxie's Pawnshop on Main Street?" Daddy got up, looked under the kitchen sink, pulled out the garbage sack. He set it by his chair and used it for an ashtray. "Do you remember?"

"Vaguely," said Mama to the wall. It must have confused Grandma because she turned around and looked to see who was there.

"That old scamp Maxie, he was having a Going Out of Business sale. We really thought he was giving us a good deal." Daddy laughed a little at the joke that had been played and shook his head.

"It was a cold day," he continued, "but Maxie always kept it hot as August in that store. You had on your pink sweater, and you took it off and laid it on the back of a chair. We was like two kids, so excited about buying something big for the first time, that we run off and forgot it."

Now Mama looked at him, and the frost disappeared from the kitchen window.

"You didn't even notice until we got to the corner," Daddy added.

"I remember buying the icebox at Maxie's, but I don't remember forgetting my sweater," she said.

"You ain't got no reason to remember that part, but I do." Daddy flicked his ashes in the sack again.

Now what was going on? Why had he walked in here and launched into this sappy story about a pink sweater? I looked at the others. Mama was idling in neutral. Spencer was pushing a bean across his plate. Grandma was listening to the story, but her mind was missing as many pieces as a leftover jigsaw puzzle.

A tiny window in the back of my brain opened, and a little voice whispered, your daddy is trying to apologize to your mama. Your daddy is sorry he ran out. Could that be true? He certainly was peaked looking. But I had never heard him apologize before, not even when he broke her nose. He had always claimed he owned us and the air we breathed. When had he ever needed Mama's forgiveness for anything? Then the little voice spoke once more before the tiny window closed. It whispered *things have changed; this time your daddy is afraid.*

I shook my head. He had never backed down from anything: not going to work on the coldest winter morning when it was still dark outside, not the big boss who drove the white Cadillac and wore a diamond horseshoe on his pinkie, not the meanest bully on the dock, not the black Doberman down the block. He couldn't be scared of my pixie mama who was only five feet one and a half inches tall except now that she wore her hair bowling ball style, she was at least five feet four.

Daddy went on with his story. "I told you to wait, and I ran back in. The sweater was missing from where you left it. I asked Maxie, 'Where's my wife's sweater?' He found it for me, and I went back to where you were and put it over your shoulders."

"I still don't remember," Mama said.

Daddy told her, "Well, I remember because it was the first time I'd ever said, 'My wife.'"

Mama seemed to be tasting his words.

"I was a proud man that day."

"That's a nice story, Charlie." She picked up her glass and swallowed the last of the ice tea, and then she reached across the table and stacked the plates.

"Maxie's still open," Daddy added.

In a minute, Mama was going to say, *well, Charlie, we ate all the beans, but I could thaw out some hamburger meat.* Then she'd hop up and start cooking, and the missing three weeks would not be mentioned until the next time he stomped out of the house. She'd tell Spencer and me to hush if we asked questions.

"I used to have me a good old icebox," Grandma said, "it was a dandy."

"You already said that once, Mother."

"Well, I never did." Grandma stuck out her bony old bird cage. "I just now mentioned it."

"I need to go finish my homework." Spencer looked at Mama to see if all systems were go.

Mama nodded and finished clearing the table except for the box of candy. Daddy had been bringing her chocolate covered cherries for as long as I could remember. They were her favorite candy just like Sophisticated Lady was her favorite scent. Daddy loved it when she got fixed up and sashayed into the living room in a cloud of her signature perfume. He'd go over and bury his face in her neck, and his hands would start moving over her body.

"I've got Roman hands and Russian fingers!" he'd always growl then throw his head back and howl like the Wolfman.

Spencer and me would look at each other like *what the heck?* Daddy would try to pick Mama up then and carry her into the bedroom. She'd push him away, but her pink face would tell us there was more there than we could figure out. It had been a long time since we had witnessed something like that, maybe years. Still, I remembered.

But in the kitchen before we could go about the business of the night, the icebox cut out again.

"I'll go get my toolbox out of the car." Daddy started to get up.

Mama said, "Leave it."

He sat back down.

She carried the stack of dishes to the sink then walked back to the table.

"Jesus will take care of it. That icebox is in his hands. Just like we all are." Mama raised her chin in the air.

The water pooled under the icebox and ran across the floor. Daddy had to lift his feet out of the way.

"Well, your Jesus better get busy 'cause we're fixing to have us a flood." He gave a little laugh still holding his feet up.

"That is my Lord and Savior you are cracking jokes about." She closed the lid on the bean pot harder than she needed to.

Daddy realized his mistake. He put his feet down in the water and looked at her, probably to see how much damage had been done.

She turned to me. "Martha, start on these dishes. Spencer, help your grandmother get ready for bed."

"Yes ma'am."

We didn't need to be told twice. I slopped through the water to the sink and started on the supper dishes. Spencer and Grandma split.

"What is this?" she asked Daddy. I glanced over my shoulder. She held the box of candy, turning it over and over in her hand as if she hadn't seen a hundred just like it.

"Chocolate-covered cherries. Your favorite." Daddy said, sounding grateful for his ace in the hole.

Mama said, "Turtles."

Daddy asked, "Turtles?"

Mama went on and her voice grew louder. "Turtles is my favorite. Pecans and caramel covered with milk chocolate. In the shape of a little turtle. Those have always been my favorite."

Daddy's cigarette lighter clicked open, then shut. Open, shut. Open. Shut.

"Why what do you mean, Pixie? I been bringing you this kind of candy since we was in high school."

Mama's voice turned shrill.

"I hate chocolate-covered cherries. I hated them in high school, too. And you'd know that if you ever paid any attention. I never ate more than one. One out of the whole box and then just to be polite. You and the kids always ate the rest."

"Now, Sweetie Pie," Daddy said, "I've been gone for three weeks. Surely you're not going to pick a fight over a box of candy?"

A loud noise hit the garbage sack, and again I turned to look. Mama had chucked the candy from all the way across the room.

Somewhere in the house a door opened, and a cold draft blew across the wet kitchen floor. It chilled me to the bone.

"No, I'm not going to pick a fight over a box of candy." Her free throw had caused her bowling ball of hair to slip a little, and she reached up and set it back in place. "What I want to know is where have you been the last three weeks?"

Daddy, his face dark and twisted, rose from his chair and walked toward Mama.

The kitchen window frosted over.

Chapter Eight
Sentimental Journey, 1970

A song played in the back of my brain.

It was just out of reach. No matter what I was doing that day the song was always there, teasing me. It had probably started at school when the teachers let us play records, but maybe it began before that. I couldn't quite catch the words of the song, and it kept scratching at my door like a nuisance cat wanting to be let in. Really getting on my last nerve.

It was the day before Thanksgiving, and the teachers knew no child was going to concentrate on the gross national product of Chile, the division of fractions, or how to handle a dangling participle. They let us goof off all day. The girls with hips hovered by the record player, and every now and then a boy walked over and punched one in the arm. Her voice would go high, and she'd lick her lips and glow. The girls without hips went outside and played in the ditch. The girls with big hips hid in the supply closet, gnawed at their wrists, and lied about how none of it mattered.

I heard them whispering.

Spoon and me sat in the back of the room and amused ourselves with tic-tac-toe and hangman. She had the right-sized hips, but she was one of them Holy Rolling Spoon girls. I was starting to get hips, but if I had gone near the record player, the top girls would have clawed me to death. I could have gone outside and jumped in the ditch and sailed a little boat downstream, but I always stuck with the Spoon.

Better-dead-than-red-on-the-head Shelby sauntered to the back of the room. Most boys, I couldn't stand. They were fun to play catch with, but it wasn't like you could have a conversation. I had an easy time with Shelby, though, since I had known him forever. He was my main source of ocean facts and figures. Shelby had dreams, like me. He was going to escape, too, and go places. Maybe all the way to California. He had developed a mad crush on Spoon this year, but she ignored him. She hated everyone in the class except for me.

"Hey, girls," he said.

"Hi, Shelby." That was me.

Spoon said *nada.*

Shelby sat down at an empty desk. He had nothing to lose being seen with us since he was not part of any group either.

"Y'all having a big Thanksgiving?" he asked.

"My daddy's gone," I answered, and for just a second the song in my head danced closer. "For good. We think." I chewed a fingernail.

Shelby hadn't even heard. He talked to me, but looked at Spoon. She pushed her pencil hard for the x in tic-tac-toe, and the lead broke. Then she gave a huge yawn right in Shelby's face and laid her head down on her arm and gave a fake snore.

Shelby stared at her for seven seconds. Then he tugged the paper out from under Spoon's arm, and we finished the tic-tac-toe game and started another one.

After an eternity, the last bell of the day rang. Spoon wiped the drool off her cheek, and we headed for the door. Shelby got lost in the crowd. We met up with Spencer and the two little Spoons in front of their school. The freedom of the day must have gone to Spencer's head. He pretended to machine gun everyone in his path, *rat-a-tat-tat-tat.* The girls ignored him, walking along dragging their coats on the ground. I took off my sweater and tied it around my waist. People said the weather had been messed up ever since last year when Neil Armstrong walked on the moon and interfered with natural law. God will not be mocked, Sister Thelma intoned, with arms folded across her bosom, any time the subject came up.

Soon we left the school and the brick houses behind and went down the hill toward the river. Spoon kept checking over her shoulder. She didn't like Shelby and said he was a bother, but she always looked to see if he was following.

A gang of neighborhood kids was tossing a football around in a vacant lot. Someone burned leaves and smoke signals went up. Young men washed their cars while on the radio Shocking Blue proclaimed: *She's got it, yeah, baby, she's got it!/ Well I'm your Venus, I'm your fire/ at your desire.*

Over the railroad tracks, the sidewalk broke. Things began to look nastier. The train tunnel bum, an empty bottle in his hand and flies buzzing around his head, sprawled in front of the liquor store. His smell, worse than tomcat piss, threatened to pounce on us, so we pinched our noses and ran and didn't stop for awhile. Rounding a corner, the peeling paint of God's House of Whole Truth greeted us. Today the sign proclaimed: *Jesus Dyed For Your Sins!* We walked by like we didn't know it.

Spencer and the girls advanced a whole block ahead of us, so we made our move. Other kids took shortcuts home, but me and Spoon followed the route of the garbage man. We ducked into an alley. We knew which day was best for scavenging and which rotting garbage can was likely to have something delectable. Once we found a whole pile of *True Romances.* We stashed them under some bushes and visited every afternoon until the day the magazines disappeared. I'd read the good parts to Spoon in a low, sexy voice. The stories were always about a young, neglected housewife who needed the services of a repairman. He would have a twinkle in his eye, boyish grin, and a tight work uniform. Before they did the dirty deed, a little birthday candle of good sense would flare in the housewife's mind, and the rascal would be shown the back door. We never got all the details. Nevertheless, we'd howl like banshees and roll around on the ground laughing at the horny women panting over these stupid stories. Eventually, we'd get up and stagger home, dizzy with lust ourselves.

Wasted tea bags. Banana peels that had lost their slip. One woman's shoe, size ten. We stared. No woman we knew had a foot that big. The *True Romance* readers were too busy basting turkeys and making pumpkin pies to worry about taking out the good trash. We stepped out of the alley, carefully checking to make sure no one was lurking. About a half block away, Shelby leaned against a lamp post with his hands stuck in his pockets.

"Why are you following us?" yelled Spoon.

"I'm not," he yelled back, "I live on this street."

Sure enough he did. He walked by us, grinning. He was the smallest boy in our class, about my size, and we were both head and shoulders shorter than Spoon. We waited for him to get ahead before we started moving again. Shelby glanced at the street. A baby-blue Cadillac, with its lights on and its motor running, double-parked. An old lady stood on the sidewalk wearing a neck brace and holding a clipboard.

"Who is that?" Spoon asked.

"Don't know," I answered. Was she an enterprising Avon lady? Had she come down here to collect rent money?

"Probation officer, you think?" offered Spoon.

"Wait a second!" I exclaimed. "It's the principal from the elementary school."

"What's that witch doing in this neighborhood?" Spoon stopped dead in her tracks.

A young guy in blue jeans hustled a bushel basket of food out of the trunk of the Caddy and ran it up to the nearest house, but you could tell the principal was in charge, her shoulders as square as the clipboard. The guy was just there for muscle.

We checked her out.

She wore an orange dress with little brown turkeys all over it. The old girl had taken some of the material that the dress was made of and used it to cover her neck brace. Still had her cat eye glasses, too, highly fashionable in 1957 and wore her hair in an old-fashioned bun. High heels with buckles across the toe, like something Miles Standish would wear. A cluster of jewels shone on her yeasty bosom.

Spoon grabbed my hand. "Shoot me if I ever dress like that."

I crossed my heart and hoped to die; I pledged to stick a thousand needles in my eye if I ever let her out of the house dressed like that.

The guy hopped into the driver's seat. The principal, moving slower than I had ever seen, got in on the passenger side. She turned her whole body toward the fellow and gave him his next instructions. She never spoke to me again after the coat incident in the fifth grade. I held a moment of silence for the loss of the panther coat with the leopard spot collar, the only chance I ever got to look like a girl from Paris, France. The only chance so far, I amended.

We passed the porch where they left the bushel basket of Thanksgiving goodies. I was positive that the lady of the house wouldn't want to be seen taking the food. Sure enough, the door opened a crack and a small hand, commissioned by its mother, crept out the door toward the stuff.

"I'd never take their charity," sniffed Spoon. This came from a girl who was having turkey and dressing for Thanksgiving. And corn on the cob and mashed potatoes with brown gravy. And cranberry sauce. And a casserole made of green beans, cream of mushroom soup, and a can of french fried onion rings sprinkled on the top. Hot rolls. Three kinds of pie. I had been hearing these details for a week or two now. Brother Spoon had taken on a second job, and the family was flush.

We had been on a menu of pinto beans and fried potatoes for quite awhile now. Grandma's check was buying the groceries, and it didn't go far. "I don't see anything wrong with accepting the food if you're hungry," I told Spoon.

"We took a basket one year," she admitted. "You'd have thought they was giving us gold. They were so puffed up about their good deed." She stepped over a broken place in the sidewalk. "I wish those snobs would go back up the hill and never come back down."

I wished they would leave a basket of food on my porch.

Up ahead at the corner, Shelby sat in the grass. When we got near, he stood up.

"Hey, I found something for you, Martha." He handed me a lucky clover.

"Thanks, Shelby." I slipped it into my buttonhole.

"And something for you, Sheila." With a flourish, he handed her a little bunch of green with white blossoms.

Oh, brother.

"Charming." She gave them a sniff and tossed the bunch over her shoulder.

Shelby stood there, grinning like the village idiot.

"We have to go now, Shelby," I said. "Talk to you later."

"O.K., Martha." He never stopped looking at Spoon.

I wanted to tell him it's a lost cause, *mi amigo.* She liked me and me alone. Poor Shelby. No one had worked harder since Pepé Le Pew tried to take the kitty to the Casbah.

"Do you think you could stare at someone else?" Spoon asked.

Shelby blushed, his face like a clear glass filling up with pink Koolaid. A vein bulged in his forehead.

It was fascinating to watch.

"Sorry," he answered. "Most girls like to get flowers."

"We ain't most girls." Spoon threw her arm over my shoulders.

We moved past Shelby, and I smiled, meaning no hard feelings. He looked sad but smiled back, the feeble look of a soldier trying to be brave. The song that had been playing in the back of my mind came so close then. I probably would have caught it except I looked up and saw trouble rolling down the street.

Shelby's big mother. Red-headed like him with biceps like canned hams, she was the meanest woman in the neighborhood and believed it her Christian duty to discipline her children and everybody else's by knocking their heads together. Sometimes parents sent thank-you notes; sometimes they filed a suit depending on how much damage was done. Right then she bore down on us like a bowling bowl about to strike. Spoon and me quickly stepped to the side. In two seconds, she had Shelby in a headlock and was dragging him down the sidewalk. All the time, he cried, "I'm sorry, Ma."

"I told you," she yelled, "I told you not to be late."

Me and Spoon crossed the street. No one wanted to watch the spectacle of a almost grown child being lynched by his mother.

The Cadillac drove slowly by, and the occupants gawked at Shelby and his ma. My face washed pink. It was one thing for me and Spoon to see Shelby's embarrassment. We were used to his big mother and had our own heads in her vise-like grip at one time or another. A much worse humiliation when the enemy witnessed it. Then, I wished they would hurry and get back up the hill, too.

Spoon went straight and followed her sisters home. A radio, sitting in an open window, played Sly and the Family Stone: *I want to take you high-er.* I cut through a backyard or two until, finally, I was on my street. The baby-blue Caddy beat me there. The principal lingered on the sidewalk, staring up at my house. Her young slave deposited the basket and skipped back down the steps to the Caddy.

Grandma stood on the porch watching the action. Spencer dived into the bushel basket of food, stacking up cans on the porch. He could have at least waited until they had driven off, so it wouldn't look like we were starving to death.

I wondered what the principal was gawking at, then I looked through her eyes.

Grandma wore overalls, one strap unhitched. They were filthy with dirt. What had she been into that day? Her hair was all Einsteined out. She hated for anyone to touch it, so we didn't usually. She had no meat on her bones and no shoes on her feet. Snuff juice dribbled down her chin. Poor Grandma.

"There, but for the grace of God, go I," said the principal to herself. Her eyes were magnified and glowing behind the glasses. She had smugness all over her face, and she licked it away like a cat licking cream from its whiskers.

I did not think she really believed in the grace of God. She believed she was better than us, just like she always had.

Stinging anger came at me. My temperature shot up to 103 degrees.

She didn't even notice me until I walked up the stairs and stood beside Grandma.

"Oh," the principal said, "Is this your house, Martha?"

"This is my house," I said. "And this is my grandmother." I reached for Grandma's hand. She started swinging our arms back and forth, like we were little girls. I gave the principal a kryptonite stare.

She hesitated. "I grew up a few blocks from here."

I didn't say a word.

The principal woman's hand went to her hair, and she pushed a strand back into place.

Grandma swung harder.

I gave the principal a second helping of the stare which wasn't easy to do since Grandma was about to jerk my arm out of its socket.

The principal touched her neck brace. She looked down at her clipboard. I was getting to her. I could tell.

Later, when I told the story to Spoon, she would say, *show me that stare one more time, Martha.*

The principal tried again: "How do you like middle school?"

Not nearly as much as I liked watching her sweat.

"Eureka!" Spencer shouted and grabbed our attention. He dug Froot Loops out from the bottom of the basket.

I let go of Grandma and went to kick the cereal off the porch. Spencer saw the hard look on my face, though, and he hugged the box to his chest.

"Mine," he said, "all mine."

God, he was a wormy little kid.

Right about that time a car honked. Sister Thelma's big car with fins was slowly backing down the street. Her transmission had gotten stuck in reverse, and she couldn't get it fixed until payday and maybe not even then. Watching her try to park was like watching a spaceship land. Inside the car, Mama rode shotgun. She was smiling, but Sister Thelma was laughing so hard her bowling ball of hair bounced around. Sometimes she didn't act like a Holy Rolling toilet bowl cleaner. They got out of the car, and Mama carried a sack of groceries with a big bunch of greens spilling out of it. Greens for Thanksgiving. Yum. Yum.

They nodded politely to the principal and walked up the steps to the porch. Then Mama noticed the food basket. Spencer was ripping into the cereal box.

"Spencer, what do you have?"

Like the thief in the night who hears the bark of a dog, he froze.

"It's just a little something the children collected at school," the principal said. "Your house was identified as one that might be needing some extra here at this time of Thanksgiving." She tapped the clipboard with a long red fingernail.

Mama glanced at the principal, then stared at the food. I knew she wanted to deny that we needed any extra at Thanksgiving or any other time. She didn't want a bushel basket of canned charity. She wanted her own table groaning with pleasure and a good husband, leaning back in his chair with a toothpick in his mouth, full and satisfied with what he had provided.

"Can we keep it, Mama?" asked Spencer.

But there was no husband here, and her Spencer hardly ever asked for anything. He was not a normal child that way. Mama looked at Sister Thelma who stood back in the shadows of the porch. Sister Thelma widened her eyes. They were communicating telepathically, but I wasn't on their wavelength.

We all stood there silently.

Spencer blinked his big begging cowlashes.

Grandma pointed at the principal. "Is that one of them church heifers?"

"Thank you," Mama said to the principal, "please tell the children we appreciate it."

The principal nodded. She took one more long look at all of us. Her young slave slammed the lid of the trunk and got behind the wheel of the car. Still the woman made no move to leave.

"You've got your hands full, don't you?" The principal said to Mama. "These kids and your mother and your husband leaving you and all."

Mama jerked like she had been pushed by an invisible hand.

"Let me give you my phone number," said the principal, "if you ever need someone to talk to." She fumbled in her bag.

Mama was caught in a trap. The principal had given us a food basket, and when you take handouts from people, you have to take whatever else they wanted to hand out with it. That was the rule. Mama couldn't say, o.k., you left us the food, now get the hell out.

The principal hadn't noticed that Mama wasn't jumping on her offer. She scribbled on a scrap of paper, walked up the steps toward us, handed Mama her phone number.

"My husband left me, too," she said simply. "Years ago."

For a moment, she seemed different. I saw her sitting in the moonlight of her lamp, sewing her dress material onto the neck brace. I saw her thinking that the little kids would like her outfit. She did not know how dumb she looked. What had happened to the neck? My hate of her wavered.

Then I remembered how small she always made me feel. I remembered the Paris coat. Sister Thelma took charge. She moved from out of the shadows and said in her strong preacher voice: "With the help of the Good Lord, everything in this house is under control."

I stepped out of the way.

Any second now, the holy ghost was going to fly up Sister Thelma's skirt and explode, and she would spaz across the porch. That'd be something the principal could take back up the hill.

"We have everything we need here!" Sister Thelma declared. "Because God has been so good to us! Do I hear a-men?"

Everybody on the porch said a-men, even the nonbelievers.

The sun caught Sister Thelma's high heel yellow daffodils, and they became like a magnifying glass, shooting out a laser beam of light.

I liked this much better.

The light hit the principal in the face, and she covered her eyes like a vampire. She aged a hundred years in three seconds. Her bun exploded. It was all hideous and lovely. She hissed and showed her claws and slunk as low as someone could who was wearing a neck brace. She crawled into the front seat of the blue Caddy. Her slave threw it in gear, and they burned rubber.

Spencer went in the house and ate an early supper: three bowls of Froot Loops with three tablespoons of sugar added to each one. All doped up, he hid in the neighbor man's bushes.

Me and Grandma sat on the front steps and daintily picked at a bag of mini-marshmallows.

The bushes shook.

"What's that boy doing over there, Pixie?" Grandma asked.

"He's peeping in the neighbor's window and watching *Hogan's Heroes* on the television."

"Oh." She smiled and ate another marshmallow.

I raised my voice a little.

"Spencer, have you backslid?"

"Pshaw!" answered the bushes.

Grandma and me laughed a little, and she patted my arm. She had not gotten crazy enough to forget love. For the first time all day, my shoulders relaxed. In the west, the sun bumped his bucket on the hill, and yellow spilled down my street. The last red rose growing beside the front door turned blood velvet.

The song that had been in the back of my brain made itself known. We sang it on a Thanksgiving day when my daddy had won a free turkey. He was the one to cook it, since everybody knew the best chefs of Europe were men. He made a big fuss about the responsibility and got up early and put on one of Mama's aprons, the pink one with ruffles, the one she said was too fancy to cook in, and she was saving it for a day that hadn't come.

He stuffed the bird with cornbread and basted it and checked his watch and bragged about how good it was going to be. Mama stayed in bed and read magazines. Me and baby Spencer played with cars under the kitchen table while the old icebox kept time. My mouth started watering as soon as the smells drifted through the house. We had the table set and the salad made and the ice tea poured two hours early. Daddy retired to the living room and watched football on his little t.v. set, just like I heard other family men did on Thanksgiving all across the United States of America. He got distracted by the game and forgot to check on the turkey until smoke came pouring out of the oven. The turkey was black on the outside and raw ice in the middle and not even a slice could be salvaged.

We had all gathered around the burnt bird and stared.

Daddy stood there rubbing the back of his neck, looking confused.

Mama and Spencer and me didn't know what was going to happen next.

Then Daddy had laughed, and it was a warm laugh with no teeth in it. Then Mama laughed, too. Then Spencer. Then me.

That was the song I had been hearing all day.

The song we sang the day Daddy burned the turkey, then grandly offered to take us to the All Night Cafe for doughnuts and milk coffee. He threatened to wear Mama's pink apron. Baby Spencer chased him down the street trying to untie it. Mama and me had followed behind them giggling, and she put her arm around my shoulders. That was the song I had been hearing all day, the song we sang the day Daddy burned the turkey, back when Mama still wore her hair in a ponytail.

Chapter Nine

The Weatherman Promised Snow, 1971

One dreary Sunday afternoon in February, the weatherman promised snow. The city had no money for a plow used only once a decade, so schools would close and the buses wouldn't run. None of the men would have to clock in unless they worked for the power company. If snow came in the night, the neighbor women would sit around their kitchen tables all the next morning, drinking coffee and telling stories on each other while husbands slept late. Babies would pad around in their pajama feet and not get dressed all day. Big kids would snowball fight and build forts and beg their mamas for the sugar and vanilla needed for snow cream. Whole families, including grandparents, would forget dignity and punch cardboard boxes into sleds and head for the nearest hill. All through the day, people who never stopped for anything would slow and go to the window and watch the holiday snowflakes fall.

It was so cold in the house that I could see my breath. I dragged Daddy's old recliner over to the gas stove and settled down to wait for Spoon. Her parents always let her come over and stay with me when Mama worked all night. Mama and Spencer had just left a minute ago for the Waffle Hut, the one over by the freeway. She waited tables there now and worked in Sister Thelma's housecleaning business by day. It turned out she did know how to scrub a stranger's toilet after all.

Mama said they wouldn't have many customers this night considering the forecast, but maybe a midnight rider would stop in for two overeasy and a steak strip. Spencer always went with her in case one of the lonesome coffee drinkers got fresh. Spencer prepared Bible verses to quote at the letch until he shriveled up and crept away. When it got late, Spencer made a bed in the back booth with his coat folded for a pillow, and his feet hanging off the end of the seat.

I didn't think Mama should go to work considering what we had done that day, but she said the rent was due, and the landlord won't care what we done.

I curled up in Daddy's crappy old chair. It still smelled like him. The arms were dirty with grease and the seat cushion was flat, but it had always been his favorite, and no one else was allowed to sit in it. How many times had he sat here in this chair, chewing on the inside of his jaw and impatiently jiggling his foot? Daddy had been gone now for months. We had all admitted one by one that he wasn't coming back this time. Sometimes he sent a money order with a scribbled note stuffed in the envelope. Always postmarked from Texas or California for he was a long distance driver now. Once an envelope arrived from potato Idaho, a place so far away and foreign that we thought it existed only on maps, but, evidently, you could mail a letter from there. Oh, your daddy said hello, Mama'd say after she read the note, as if it were polite greetings from a second cousin's married daughter. Spencer would always want to know what the rest of the note said, but not me. I didn't care. I didn't have even an ounce of curiosity. Not a teaspoon of curiosity. Not a molecule of curiosity. None. Nada. Zip. Zilch. Zero.

Once when I sat here in his chair, I overheard Mama and Daddy talking. They were in the kitchen, him eating another late supper.

"I seen a girl today, Pixie, looked just like Martha," he had murmured. "Saw her from the back when I was driving down the street. She had Martha's brown hair. Even had Martha's walk. Then when I passed by, I could see it wasn't her. But she sure looked like Martha."

Mama answered back something I couldn't hear.

I didn't know my daddy had ever looked at me long enough to know I walked a certain way. I chewed on that one a long time. I had learned ages ago to stay out of rooms he was in because it was easier, but this time I wanted to ask him a question. How do I walk? I didn't know. Some things only other people can tell you about yourself. Asking him could have been a cozy little scene. He might have leaned back in his chair and taken the opportunity to hold forth for awhile. He might have lit a Camel and blown smoke rings in the air and told me that I walked like my feet were mounted on springs, or that if he had a swing like that, he'd keep it in his back yard. Or it might not have been a cozy little scene. I didn't want to take the chance.

I climbed out of the chair by the heat and went to the cold window. Mama had dishrags stuffed around all the cracks, but still the wind whistled through. My warm breath cleared away a little porthole. It was actually starting to snow; the weatherman hadn't lied. Where was Spoon? She should be turning the corner right now unless something bad had happened. She'd have on an old coat, blue jeans under her dress. A scarf that Sister Spoon made her wear, trailing from her coat pocket. A tough girl scowl spread across her face, the one she always wore walking down the street. Where was she?

Two steps away from the gas stove, and I started shivering again. I needed one of Grandma's quilts off our bed.

Outside the street lamps came on one by one, and the snow fell faster.

The empty bed was neatly made in the back. Mama straightened it this morning before we left. I saw her.

I couldn't stand at this icy window anymore, and a long cold shiver shook me.

I turned, my footsteps echoing through the house. First the wood floor, then the cracked linoleum in the kitchen, wood again, the hallway and the back room.

I stood in the doorway. The iron bed I shared with Grandma, a dresser, a fishing pole still standing in the corner, the room vacant. Grandma's wedding ring quilt covered the bed, frayed at the edges. I walked over and touched it. So soft, so worn-out. My great-grandmother had started stitching the quilt when the neighbor boy came whistling down the road one summer evening. My grandma, just a girl then, changed into a skirt and went out to join him on the porch swing. Suddenly shy, neither one could think of anything to say. Finally after five minutes that seemed five hundred, a rooster strutted by snapping at a June bug. They laughed, and the sparking began. Later the boy would become Poppy, my grandfather, who died before I was born.

I didn't remember the exact day she began talking to the dead in the distance, the day she stopped teasing Spencer, the day she stopped laughing at my dumb jokes. I do remember the day when she turned down a fishing trip to the river, the thing she liked to do best. The three of us would leave each morning, and she'd be sitting in the same chair when we came back in the afternoon, her food untouched in the icebox. When I talked, she'd stare at my face as if I were a particularly loud and rude visitor to her country. She'd blink, and I'd disappeared. Then she caught the flu and kept the cough. It got worse. We'd walk in the house and smell gas, and the stove would be on, the pilot light out. She'd pick up a lamp from the end table and take it to the gas flame as if it were kerosene and not electric. All our dreaming minutes and waking hours were haunted by the *what ifs*? Quietly, Mama and Sister Thelma started making the rounds of the nursing homes.

Spencer and me insisted we'd take turns staying home with her. But the law would get after us and that would make things worse. I wanted to ask the neighbor women to look in on Grandma, but Mama had never made any real friends among them. Disgraced after Daddy split for good, she pretended to the neighborhood that we were all fine. Even the people at God's House of Whole Truth couldn't help much as they all had their own sicknesses and debts and broken promises. They did organize a couple of prayer meetings around Daddy's return but finally conceded the devil wasn't done with him yet.

I pulled the quilt off the bed and went back to my post. Surely, Spoon would be tapping on the door any second.

When Mama first told me the nursing home she'd picked was called the Rainbow's Inn, I thought it would be a pretty place. Maybe an Irish theme with pictures on the walls of leprechauns in little green suits and pots of gold. Maybe they'd have a rule that you had to be red-headed to work there. Grandma always loved red hair. Said it was a sign of fire inside. Told me I should have been red on the head instead of brown. She said Mama should have had red hair, too, but I didn't know where she got that idea. As it turned out I was wrong about the Irish theme. There weren't any red headed workers there, not even the guy pushing the broom. No leprechauns dressed in green. At least the place was clean. Mama had stories about some of the others she'd visited that always ended with *I wouldn't put my dog in a place like that.* We spent days explaining to Grandma where she was going and why it'd be better.

Even I told that lie.

Last night the four of us had supper one more time at the kitchen table. Grandma wouldn't touch a bite of the pork chop Mama had fried special just for her. She did let me rub Vick's Salve on her chest while Spencer piled seven quilts on our bed in the back room. Grandma crawled under the warmth, and she had grown so light the iron bed didn't squeak. Spencer sat on the side of the bed and said good night. I moved around the room packing her suitcases. Mama couldn't do it. She stayed in the kitchen washing dishes and hissing *Je-sus Je-sus Je-sus* into the steam.

Spencer kept sitting there. Grandma's eyes were closed. He had his hand on top of her head like he was checking her temperature. I knew he was praying.

"Spencer."

He looked over his shoulder at me, his face so still and quiet he could have been drawn on paper.

"It's time to go to bed now."

He kissed Grandma again and left the room.

After I washed my face and changed into my gown, I climbed in beside Grandma under the quilts. Her feet were cold. We could never keep socks on her. She turned toward me.

"Martha," she whispered.

"Yes?"

"I was dreaming I was back home in my own bed with Poppy."

"You're here with me and Spencer and your daughter Pixie."

"I know where I am, Missy."

I reached under the covers until I found Grandma's hand.

"Y'all are taking me to a nursing home tomorrow."

I folded my hands around hers. "Daddy's gone, Grandma, and Mama's working two jobs. Spencer and I go to school, and there's no one here to take care of you during the day."

"I've always taken care of myself."

"I know," I said, "but you've been sick."

Grandma turned from me, but she didn't pull her hand away. She stared at the ceiling.

"I'm so sorry this is happening to us," I told her.

"What is happening to you?" she asked.

I raised up on my elbow to get a good look at her face.

"You're right," I said, "It is happening to you." I tried not to cry, and it was all I could do to hold it back. "I'd change everything if I could."

She continued to stare at the ceiling.

"Grandma..."

She took a deep breath, and the air wheezed into her tired lungs. Finally, she turned back toward me.

"It's late," she said, "go to sleep." She kissed me on the forehead. I scooted down in the bed so only the top of my head showed. I wanted to stay up all night with her, but sometime towards morning, I fell asleep and let go of my grandmother's hand.

Then the door opened, and finally the Spoon walked in brushing snow from her shoulders. She flipped on the light switch.

"Was it awful?" she asked.

"Yes."

She came over and sat on the arm of the chair. "Did she cry?"

"No. She was brave. We put her things away, then she went in the lounge and sat down and watched television like nothin' was happening. We stayed as long as we could, but Mama had to go to work."

Spoon shrugged her coat off. She leaned into the chair and put her arms around me. She smelled like the clean cold from outside.

"Poor Martha." Spoon pulled the quilt up and tucked it around me. "Is this hers?"

"I guess it's ours now."

"Is it the one her mama made when she and Poppy were sparking?"

I nodded.

Spoon traced the wedding ring pattern with her finger. Over and over. Over and over.

A little while later, we took all the quilts and made a pallet in front of the stove. We pulled the wedding ring quilt up over us since it was the favorite. Spoon put arms around me, and in the hidden darkness under the quilt, she surprised me with a kiss. A real kiss on the lips. Hers were soft and chapped. I felt so grateful; it made me want to cry. Spoon must have known I was fixing to open the floodgates.

"Hey, Bonnie," she said.

"Hey, Clyde." I smiled for the first time in days, weeks, maybe months. Bonnie and Clyde had always been our favorite outlaw game. We played it when we were ten-year-old tomboys and rode my bike to the river. It involved a lot of shooting, and bank robbing, and victory smooching. Of course, we gave all the money away to the poor widows and children. What did you need with money when you had the love and occupation of a Bonnie and Clyde? We always changed it so that the crooks escaped in the end, and the sheriff was locked up in his own jail, clanging a tin cup on the bars.

Spoon kissed me again.

"Let's pretend," she said, "we're on a train to Mexico."

"To the ocean," I said.

"On a train to the ocean, and there's a sack full of money to be spent."

"Given away."

"But," she said, "we have to buy ourselves something nice first."

"What would you buy?"

"Let me think for a minute."

We snuggled deeper under the covers, deep down in the dark. She wrapped her tough Spooner arms around me and held me there like that. I fit right under her chin.

Later we did the things we usually did and then some other things we hadn't done before, and this time, we forgot to call it a game.

When I woke up the next morning, I threw on my jeans and went to the window, longing for snow deep enough to jump in. But in the night, the snow turned to rain and everything froze. The weatherman had lied. The schools would not close. Everyone with a boss would have to clock in, for ice was not a holiday. It would all melt by noon. I watched the neighbor man go sliding down the sidewalk to his car. He couldn't get the door open, so he stood there and cursed as if his temper would thaw ice. Crystal icicles hung from all the naked trees, and one fell like a spear, crashing on the street.

I turned away from the window and looked at Spoon, curled up on her side in our bed by the stove. She peeked out from under the covers. All I could see was one brown eye, and it wasn't telling me anything.

Suddenly I felt terribly bashful. "The snow quit in the night," I said.

Spoon turned her face away and pulled the quilt over her head.

Part II

Chapter Ten

That Is the Way They Have Fun, 1973

The Spoon and I sneaked out of our houses and took the bus to uptown one Saturday morning. We were headed for the Triple Churches Yard Sale Extravaganza, and we had been earning money for it all summer. Working wasn't hard as long as you didn't mind babysitting the snot-eating neighborhood brats for fifty cents an hour or washing windows for old widow women who hadn't been satisfied with anything since 1953.

So there we were on the bus with our clutch of wrinkled dollar bills and change. It was all we could do to keep from bouncing up and down in our seats. See, in a few weeks it'd be time to start back to school, our first day of high school. This year was going to be different, a brand new start. No more embarrassment. No more shame. We were going to fit in like regular girls, and we'd figured out how to do it. The key was fashion. We were going to show up looking as good as everyone else. No, better. We'd be stunning.

The bus stopped in front of the Catholic Church, the one whose steeple threatened to puncture the sky. There were ladies flitting like butterflies and tables and tables of treasure. In the distance, Diane Bickerstaff

Buck and the Petites were selling lemonade. Spoon wanted to slip over and flip them the bird, but I was afraid they'd tell and get us kicked out. So instead we made a beeline for the clothes, and it wasn't long before we hit pay dirt. Our department store shopping bags filled up. Suddenly, we saw the most perfect piece of clothing, the one that would make all the babysitting and widow pleasing worthwhile. On a scale from one to ten with ten being the ultimate ultimate and one being your little brother's toe jam, this was at least a nine. We spotted the prize at the same moment and jerked it up from where it lay on the card table. A white cotton smock top with puffed sleeves and hand embroidered blue roses blooming across the bodice. Neither one of us would let go, and it threatened to split like King Solomon's baby. Then I noticed how the society ladies holding the yard sale were gawking at us. Their daughters were all well mannered, I supposed, so they had never seen two chicks fighting over a piece of clothing. I decided to let the Spoon have it. Better for her to have the whole blouse, than each of us with a sleeve.

Skipping away from the tables that day, we stopped for one last look before stepping off the church grounds. Someone had wheeled out a mannequin, and she was wearing a white evening gown loaded with sequins that sizzled in the sun. I pictured the mannequin with a martini and a cigarette in a holder, a half dozen love slaves gathered around her feet. If we babysat from now until we were old women, there still wouldn't be enough for that white dress. Me and Spoon stood there anyway, admiring.

"If it were yours," I asked, "where would you wear it?"

One of her black eyebrows shot up, and she thought for a minute. The society lady behind the table waited for her answer, too.

"I'd wash dishes in it!" she declared, pulling up her sleeves and pretending to scrub a plate. At the same time, she stuck her nose in the air and lowered her eyelashes.

I laughed, always appreciating Spoon's way of turning things upside down.

But the lady didn't care for Spoon's attitude, and to show it, she arranged her mouth in a harelip.

We gave one last look of longing for the dress and ran away from the tables, armed with our shopping bags, and caught the bus going back down the hill.

The plan was to stash our new clothing in the neighbor man's tool shed. We'd meet there every morning and get dressed for school. If that didn't work out, we'd keep the stuff at the number two sister's house since she lived just around the corner. That was right. Sheila was now the senior daughter over at the Spoon prison. When the number two sister turned fifteen, she had got down to featherweight for mating purposes and snagged a working man. The girl had a lazy eye along with being substantial, and Daddy Spoon claimed it was only his prayers that delivered her a husband. It'll be back to butt city before the ink dries on the wedding license, Spoon had told me and we cackled. This sister was coming in handy though as her home was a place we could go hang out. Since she had escaped the domination of her father, Number Two had taken up all kinds of vices: card-playing, cigarette smoking, beer drinking. She had a stack of *True Romance* magazines.

Late one afternoon in her living room, she taught us the French inhale where you filled your mouth like a tea cup, then slowly sucked the smoke up your nose. I didn't know where the smoke went after that because we never got past the sucking up part. Her new husband had stumbled in the back door with his empty lunch pail banging against his knee and a quart of Pabst Blue Ribbon in a brown paper bag. His name was Junior. He was so terribly skinny that the neighborhood women were always slipping Number Two their secret cake recipes. So far he hadn't gained an ounce, although Number Two made a cake every payday. Junior slumped over the kitchen sink and scrubbed at the grease on his hands that would probably be there when they closed his coffin lid. Number Two got fancy and poured the beer in glasses and even let me and Spoon have a swallow. It tasted awful, but I smiled and proposed a toast to the newlyweds. That seemed to turn Junior's mood. He rubbed Number Two's fanny and pronounced her his little Sugar Puddin'. Then he sat in his easy chair and taught us a card game called "Fuck Your Buddy" that he had learned one night in the drunk tank.

The day finally came for our conquest of this new world, Jefferson Davis High School. It was the only game in town as there were several middle schools, but only one high school. Spoon and her two little sisters arrived early that first morning. Spencer blew through the door and off the porch. The ghost of Sweet Pea came through the bushes, jumping up and down and wagging her tail. She ran in circles around Spencer, but he couldn't see her.

The little girls followed closely behind Spencer. At the corner, he paused, cocked his leg, and pulled at a wedgie. The young Spoons braked, but not quickly enough, and they crashed. Sweet Pea barked silently and wagged her tail at the show.

In the tool shed, Spoon picked the blue roses out of the cardboard box and pulled it on over her head. The blouse had been starched so many times it could have trucked to school by itself. She put on a Pentecostal skirt, and through the miraculous healing power of the elastic waistband, it became a mini. We had spent some time sewing these skirts over the summer. Sister Spoon was proud of Sheila, but when my mama saw me with a sewing needle in my fingers, she walked over and put her palm against my forehead.

"The boots," said the Spoon, and she slid on a pair formerly owned by a cosmic cowgirl. Red leather. Well worn but shined to a high gloss. She had polished for hours, and a four star general couldn't have found fault with them. "How do I look?"

"Really cool," I said.

"My skirt's not too short?"

"No. Just right." Lax clothing laws ruled at Jeff Davis compared to middle school, but it was better not to attract the attention of the principal man. He stalked the halls carrying a billy club for the overgrown boys and a tape measure for the outlaw girls. Rumor had it that just a touch of his finger on a girl's thigh was enough to freeze dry all her female parts.

Hip huggers graced my hips with bell-bottom legs as wide as a doorway. Carefully ironed seams. A white poet's blouse with long, loopy sleeves and a ruffly collar. Holding my arms out, I turned around in a circle. I knew the blouse had come straight off the back of a girl hippie who sold daisies on street corners in San Francisco. Wearing this blouse would cause rhyming words to flow from my mouth all day long.

I cocked my hip and flashed Spoon the peace sign.

"You look great, too," Spoon said.

A cracked mirror leaned against one wall, and she applied mascara and eyeliner and blue eye shadow.

"Not too heavy," I cautioned. "They'll call you a whore."

"I don't know any whores," she said.

"I don't either, but that's how people talk." I pushed her away from the mirror and lacquered on the eye shadow.

Hanging on a hook at the back of the shed, Spoon retrieved a red maxi coat that matched her boots. With that, we were set. It didn't matter to her that it was supposed to get up to ninety-seven that day. We stepped out of the tool shed and closed the door. All the way to school, our footsteps kept time on the busted sidewalk. Hope was in every move we made.

The smoking hole was just this side of Jeff Davis, and we paused there for a breath like an actor before going on stage. All the teenagers from our neighborhood hung out there in the morning, and some said *hey* when we walked up. So far, so good. A lone boy pulled himself away from the wall, Shelby. He hadn't been able to join any groups either because there were three strikes against him. First, he was a known book reader. Secondly, no one else around here had a name like Shelby, and some suspected it was a pussy name. And the third strike? Pink easily blushed his pale cheeks. That kind of skin was considered essential on a girl, but on a boy, it was certain death.

"Check it out," said Shelby. "Y'all look righteous." He placed one hand over his heart and pretended it was pumping out of his chest.

We giggled our thanks.

Shelby had spent the summer making some improvements, too. We had seen him at a few of the yard sales, and now he had on one purple paisley shirt.

"Hey, Martha," he said, "look at this book I found." He held up a tattered paperback with the cover ripped off.

"What's it about?"

He opened it and read: "Once upon a time when the world was young there was a Martian named Valentine Michael Smith."

"Wait just a second." I said. "How could a Martian be named Smith? He should have a gobbledygook name."

"Well, you see…" he started to explain.

Spoon kicked me and Shelby saw it. Spoon said when me and him got together we always talked highbrow and left her out.

Shelby, realizing his mistake, put his book away. I'd like to know more about a Martian named Smith, but this wasn't the time. We went back to staring at everything, but the excitement and nervousness got to us, and soon we were punching each other. It was just that kind of day. Then one of the older dudes broke away from his buddies and walked over to us. He had amazing hair and a leather headband and those big Arkansas-type ears. It was too bad he couldn't do anything about his skin, which was erupting like Pompeii.

"Hey, punk," he said.

Shelby sighed and stuffed his hands in his pockets, his back to the guy. His shoulders came up as if they were already anticipating a blow. Spoon found something interesting to look at on the ground. I said a silent prayer. Shelby turned around and faced the name caller. With all the grace and dignity of a gentleman, he said, "That would be me."

"Yeah, you." The name caller flicked the hair that grew over Shelby's ears, and Shelby flinched. "What's this shit?"

Now I knew the older dude couldn't possibly object to Shelby's style since his own dish water blonde hair was halfway down his back. The name caller didn't wait for an answer.

"Listen, dude. You need to know who made this possible."

Shelby nodded.

"I'm the man who broke the hair barrier."

Shelby nodded again as if the dude was making sense.

"I walked in to Jeff Davis one fine fall day. I knew I was gonna get my ass kicked. My hair was down to here." He tapped the top of his shoulder. "The jocks and the rednecks carried me upstairs to the third floor bathroom and put my head in the toilet. Then flushed it."

Now we could figure out where this was going, and we all started to relax a little. Shelby kept nodding every few seconds while the name caller went on with his story.

"...they got out the scissors and that's when the cops had to be called. But, you know what, little buddy?"

Shelby shook his head in reply. I was pretty sure no one had ever called him "little buddy" before. I smiled.

"Hair grows!" the name caller crowed and threw his head back and laughed so hard we could count every silver filling. He put his hand out.

"Name's Dude," said the dude.

"Name's... Mike," said Shelby.

Then Dude and Shelby did that guy handshake thing where they start out with their fingers in a clench, then five minutes later they're bumping their skinny hips together. The Spoon and I rolled our eyes, but it was just for show.

"Hey, stop by sometime. We'll get high." Dude's eyes did the usual bounce from Spoon to me and back to Spoon. "Bring the chicks." He wiggled his ears.

"Where do you live?" asked Shelby.

"In that little house in the alley behind Piggly Wiggly."

By then, all the other smoking hole kids had gathered around us, and we walked strong to the schoolyard. When we got to the gate, the oldest boys parted and went toward the machine shop. The band's music shook the ground, but it couldn't drown out the last words of the Dude. He jumped high in the air and flipped the bird to everyone inside the schoolyard.

"Fuck all y'all!" he shouted with joy.

A huge pep assembly dominated the courtyard. We were going inside the school to find our lockers, but Spoon wanted to watch for awhile so we found a wall to lean against. She took off the red maxi coat and artfully arranged herself like a centerpiece, but Shelby and me just goofed.

The principal man stood to one side pounding his billy club into his hand and holding a whistle in his mouth. He blew about every ten seconds, but no one paid any attention. The band, wearing the red and gray of the Fighting Rebels, played "Dixie," and some of the teachers wiped their eyes. The pep squad goosestepped by. Hulking football players jogged around the schoolyard carrying shiny cheerleaders piggyback. The reigning Miss Junior Missy tippy toed past in a pair of her mother's high heels and a sweater set. She left a trail of perfume. I sniffed the air. Spoon said, "Love's Baby Soft." School buses lined up and dumped their loads, and the crowd swelled. There was a dizzifying amount of paisley.

"Here come the colored kids," Miss Junior Missy screeched, then wiped lipstick off her teeth.

I glanced at the sky to see if they were parachuting in, but just then an old yellow bus ground to a stop. Its front bumper fell off with a loud clang.

The door wheezed open. Out stepped a girl. She had on a starched dress with a sash, as if her mother had dressed her for Sunday school. Poor kid. Miss Junior

Missy walked toward her with her hand outstretched like she was a member of the Welcome Wagon. The girl took one look and got back on the bus. We kept watching. More of the same prissy dresses. No bell bottoms. No polyester silk shirts. No Afros. Not one platform shoe. What was the deal, we wondered, as they walked the gauntlet.

"Guess they haven't had their Summer of Love," I said.

"Like we have?" answered Spoon.

"At least we've got the clothes," said Shelby.

We sure did, patting ourselves appreciatively.

Then, finally, a reward. The last guy on the bus stepped off. His Afro so wide, he could have used a set of curb feelers.

Shelby jumped in front of the boy. He raised his fist in the Black Power salute. "Jimi Hendrix!" he screamed.

"Jimmy who?" said the kid.

"Jimi Hendrix!" Shelby fingered an imaginary guitar. He kicked into the air; he spun around; he did the splits.

The boy reached deep within his 'fro and pulled out a metal pick. He adjusted his hairdo, all the while not taking his eyes off the red-headed peckerwood.

"Star-Spangled Banner!" screamed Shelby in the guy's face, spewing spit. He pulled out his lighter and set the imaginary guitar on fire.

The kid put his pick back in its resting spot, his arm disappearing up to his elbow. Again, he tried to move past.

"Foxy Lady!" screamed Shelby.

The guy stared at Shelby like he was that nasty shit you'd find on the floor if you accidentally kicked over your grandma's spit can. He stepped toward him.

It wouldn't help Shelby's reputation to get stomped on the first day of school.

"Calm down, Shelby." I pulled him out of the way. He was panting.

The guy shook his head to clear it, and the crowd ate him up.

But we couldn't calm down, and we couldn't stop smiling like lunatics. Shelby kept playing his imaginary guitar. Spoon rolled her eyes so far back in her head she looked demon possessed.

The first bell rang and most turned like a herd of cattle toward the front door. Miss Junior Missy polished her tiara and secured it in a leather case. The cheerleaders slid off the backs of the football players. The band put away their instruments. It was going to be a beautiful day. The sun was shining everywhere, and some of its rays touched us. We belonged here.

Then Shelby nudged me and pointed to the street with his chin. It was none other than the fabulous Diane Bickerstaff Buck arriving in her mother's wood paneled station wagon. The girls she owned jumped up and down like they hadn't seen her in years, and they rushed the car. Spoon put her finger in her mouth and pretended to vomit. Diane stepped out and tossed her glistening blonde hair over one shoulder. She was wearing a lime green mini-dress and orange fishnet stockings. With every step, her little skirt bounced. All the boys swallowed their tongues. Within one week, this blondie would be a cheerleader, an honor never before purchased by a ninth grader. The Queen and her ladies-in-waiting crossed the street and entered the courtyard.

Then the unthinkable happened right there in front of us.

The Queen stumbled.

The ladies tried to catch her, but they moved in slow motion. Someone had left a backpack in her path, and she tripped over it and went down just like a commoner would have. For a second, it was orange fishnet stockings, white panties, and possum flying through the air, then Diane sprawled on the ground. All the ladies-in-waiting gathered around her, and the second-in-command screamed.

"Medic!"

The principal shoved through the crowd. Diane had a scratch on her knee, and he ran for the first aid kit. The people gawked, and a strange embarrassed silence fell. But none of this was the unthinkable. It happened next.

The Spoon laughed. Not a little giggle behind the hand, not a "this is just for us" chuckle, but a laugh that cracked the air like a home run baseball. Everyone heard it.

Diane's mouth twisted ugly.

"Help me," she commanded, and the blondies pulled her up. She stood in front of us in three seconds flat. Shelby and me stood behind Spoon and looked over her shoulder. I couldn't believe she was doing this. We had gotten bigger in our new clothes but not big enough for this challenge.

Diane stood there with her hands on her hips. Her eyes shifted, and I knew she was taking a good look at the new, improved Spoon: the red cowgirl boots, the long bare legs, the mini-skirt, the blue roses blooming.

Her eyes rested on the roses. She started nodding.

"That's my sister's blouse."

"I bought it at the church sale," countered Spoon.

"She did," I agreed. "I was with her."

Diane went on as if we had never spoken. "Just wait until I tell my sister that the white trash holy rolling Spoon girl is wearing her shirt. She'll just die!"

And with that, it all began again.

The three of us met at the flagpole after school, our heads hanging down. When I walked into Algebra, the teacher, Mrs. Piercy, looked me up and down and sniffed. She made me go sit in the office until the secretary checked my records. My advanced placement was not an error. Back in the classroom, Mrs. Piercy stood over my shoulder and every time I made a mistake, she bopped me on top of the head with her pencil. I didn't understand. Most of the school dressed just like me. How did Mrs. Piercy know I was from down by the river? What was it about living there meant I couldn't be good in math? I felt like I must be marked, like I had been pissed on by a dog.

My friends shook their heads sadly, then told their stories.

Shelby had been forced to climb a rope by a large stinky man who chewed a wet cigar.

The principal measured the Spoon.

"I tried to fit in, Martha, I really did," she said.

I had tried, too. We all had. The three of us just stood there looking at each other, the stink of disappointment all over us.

Then Spoon pulled out her hairbrush and started stroking her hair. "I know what," she said, "let's go to the House in the Alley."

It turned out that I didn't have any classes with Spoon, so I hadn't talked to her much that day. She hadn't said anything at lunch.

"That Dude sure was cute." Spoon looked at me defiantly.

So *he* was on her mind.

"Nice, too," said Shelby, "he shook my hand."

"I told Mama I'd go see my grandma after school. She has pneumonia again. Mama'll pitch a fit if I don't go."

"We won't stay long," Spoon said.

She was always getting crushes on one boy or the other. I had gotten used to it. Once it was a stringy haired guy standing on the street corner with a cigarette stuck on his lip and a rough look on his moon crater face. She had talked about him for days. When it got to be too aggravating, I'd reminded her that these boys used to torture the Spoon girls, and she had probably beaten up half of 'em. That shut her up.

Dude hadn't paid any special attention to me. Guys never did when I was standing next to Spoon. I had all the same parts she did. Hers was just bigger. One day when some of the church women were at the house, Mama had said, *when I was Martha's age, I was already wearing a B cup.* They all looked at me accusingly as if I were growing my tits slowly just to spite them. But then the usually quiet Sister Spoon spoke: *She's lucky, maybe they'll leave her alone, and she'll get to have more time for herself.* Everyone in the room had stared; no one was used to hearing a woman talk about a girl needing time. Especially from a woman who signed so quickly for her underage daughters to marry.

"Yeah, Martha, we'll just stay for a minute," Shelby added, pulling my mind back to the flagpole.

He pulled a hairbrush from his back pocket and went to work on his fair head. They turned away as if it were settled and started weaving their way through the crowd. I had to hurry to catch up.

We stood at the entrance of the alley, Shelby and Spoon and me.

"Here, kitty, kitty, kitty," I called.

Shelby looked puzzled. Spoon slapped my arm.

"Don't do anything uncool," she said.

Spoon took her coat off and draped it over her shoulders. "I wish I hadn't worn this thing. It's too hot. Does it look stupid with me wearing it like this?"

"Yes," I answered.

She punched me again.

"Damn it, would you stop hitting me!"

"I'm sorry," she answered, "I always hit people when I'm nervous." She rolled up her skirt about six inches. "Is this too short?"

"Yes," I answered.

"No," said Shelby at the same time. He ran the brush through his hair again. "Y'all ready?"

Nobody answered. Nobody moved.

I made another attempt to change their minds.

"Listen, we could go hang out at my house. Mama's working and Spencer is with her."

They didn't bother to answer, just kept looking down the alley.

"Are we ready for California people?" I asked.

"Dude's from around here somewhere," said Spoon. "I've seen him before."

"Yeah," I said, "those pimples would be hard to forget."

That earned me an iceberg stare.

I made a face at her.

"I hope your face gets stuck that way," she said.

"Me and you both."

Still we stood there.

Spoon nudged Shelby. "You're the guy. You go first."

"Fuck that," he answered.

She released a heavy sigh. Shaking us off, she walked into the alley. After a few steps, she turned back and looked at us, "What could go wrong after today, anyhow?"

My and Shelby's sneakers didn't make any noise, but Spoon's cowgirl boots tapped tapped tapped past the sycamore trees and the spiky pompoms on the ground, past the stinking dumpster and its family of alley cats, past a barking dog behind a wooden fence.

We smelled that strange smell first.

"Remember my name is Mike," said Shelby.

Then we walked over the rise and down into the little valley, and it was too late to turn back.

We were there.

The furniture rested outside. A green plaid couch piled with junk was over by the trash can. A man wearing a brace sat in an easy chair with his bum leg propped on the coffee table. He finished a beer and threw the can over his shoulder toward the garbage. A tall frizzy haired chick stood at the kitchen table making sandwiches from a block of commodity cheese. She was wearing a purple bedspread. Must have been the California influence. I heard Mama's voice: *A little Dippity-Do and that hair'd be gorgeous!* Tall speakers from the stereo were on the porch, and the woman singer was begging for mercy: *Didn't I make you feel/ like you were the only one?* Her voice held the misery of a cat-in-heat locked in the back room. Some guys slumped in the kitchen chairs, and they passed around a pink cigarette. They glanced at us, but nobody got excited or anything.

Shelby cleared his throat. "Hey, Dude around this afternoon?"

The tall girl with the hair looked up.

"Sure," she said, "come on in."

We walked through what we hoped was the front door of the outside house. I tripped over the threshold that wasn't there. Then I almost tripped over a baby girl who was there, sitting in the living room yard eating grass. The screen door slammed on the real house, and the Dude himself appeared on the porch. No shirt, blue jeans, bare feet.

"Hey, foxy mamas!"

Spoon and me said "hey" back.

"Hey, little buddy!"

Shelby smiled.

"Y'all have a seat," Dude invited. He cleaned off the couch by tipping it up on its end. All the junk slid to the yard floor. Everyone laughed. Especially Spoon and Shelby and me. We laughed as if it were the most brilliant thing we'd ever seen. We laughed long after everyone else had stopped.

Then we sat down and shut up.

The woman singer screeched something about a *ball and chain.* The Dippity-Do girl went right on slicing cheese. The guys continued smoking. We perched on the edge of the couch. Soon the silence among us was unbearable.

"Nice place, you have here," Spoon said, using the manners her mama had taught her, "bet you don't have to sweep much."

The folks looked at her like she was loco. Nobody said a word. Spoon wilted right in front of my eyes. Dude handed Shelby a bottle of Boone's Farm, then he sat cross-legged on the ground. Shelby took a swallow and passed it to Spoon, then she passed it to me. I had a little sip. It tasted sweet like Koolaid, and I understood why there were so many empty bottles gathered around the trashcan.

The man in the leg brace checked us out. He wore an Army jacket and camouflage pants, and he had a bandana tied around his forehead. His eyes were blue and bloodshot and looked as though he'd stayed up late every night for two hundred years. He leaned forward and asked if we went to Jeff Davis.

"Yes, sir," said Shelby.

"Sir?" said the man. "Do I look like a sir?"

Shelby shook his head and this time took a big gulp of wine.

We knew that Shelby had made a mistake, but we weren't sure which kind. I wondered if this was a "three strikes and you're out" deal, and suddenly, I got a picture of Dude pushing us down the alley. And stay out, he would say, wiping his hands clean.

Then the Dippity-Do girl came over and sat down on the arm of the couch next to me.

I smiled up at her.

She smiled back.

"Want to smoke a joint?" she asked, holding the pink cigarette between two of the longest fingers I had ever seen. On a clear day, she could have reached up to heaven and picked the nose of God.

"Uh," I said.

She stuck the joint right in my face.

"Go ahead, little girl."

Everyone stared. Even the baby stopped eating grass and looked up. I'd had all the rejection I could stand for one day, so I took the joint. It wouldn't hurt this one time, and I wanted to find out what it was like. Then I heard Grandma's voice floating through the air. *Just what do you think you're doing, Missy?*

Shut up, Grandma, I answered, you wouldn't understand. They didn't have this stuff when you were a kid. I took it in slow and didn't give anyone a reason to laugh. Them smoking lessons at Number Two's really paid off. When it was Shelby's turn, he sucked it down, coughed, and the tears flowed. Dude got up and pounded him on the back. Spoon took it slow like me. With that, the show was over. The baby, a little bald-headed thing, toddled over and offered me a blade of grass. I pretended to eat. Yummy, yummy. I had half a Hershey bar in my pocket, so I broke off the pieces and fed them to her. The baby laughed and clapped her little chocolate hands for more. Did she belong to Dippity-Do?

The pot and the wine went around again and again.

A gentle breeze blew down the alley and dead leaves skittered by. Sitting outside was pleasant. Maybe I'd go home and put the couch in the front yard. The thought of what Mama would say made me giggle, and Shelby giggled, too, as if he'd read my mind, then the giggles spread around the room like cancer.

People came and went like they were changing shifts at a factory. The guy with the leg brace turned out to be a Vietnam vet, and he kept passing around a prescription bottle of pills. He tried to tell me this story about a jungle and a dark night and his best buddy, but I couldn't make any sense of it. He came over and sat on the arm of the couch by me. Suddenly, I remembered that Spoon had chores, Mama and Spencer would be home soon, and Shelby's big mother might be rolling down the street right now.

I told Shelby and Spoon we had to split. They said *right* but didn't move. Dude had gotten up, and he and Dippity-Do were exchanging karate kicks. Shelby pushed himself off the couch then, and Dude started teaching him a few licks. Spoon watched, and her eyes sparkled. The Vietnam vet picked up two sticks attached with a chain. He called them, well, it sounded like numchucks or numbnuts, and he kept throwing them up and over his shoulders and around his waist. Any second now he was going to knock himself out with the stupidest weapon I'd ever seen. These people had watched way too many Bruce Lee movies.

I turned to Spoon. It seemed like the same record had been playing for hours. This time the cat-in-heat woman was singing pretty, something about *windshield wipers keeping time/ holding Bobby's hand in mine.*

"I'm leaving when this song is over."

"O.K." Spoon never took her traitor eyes off Dude.

Oh, brother, here we go again. I wasn't moving one step without her. And what had happened to that joint? This time when the smoke poured out of my chest, the long mixed up day finally loosened its hold on me. Mrs. Piercy and her chalk fingers. The surprise on the secretary's face when she discovered my B minus average. The principal man who wanted to know what trouble I had caused when he saw me waiting outside his office. The kids with lunch money and the kids with tokens. The Stars shining and the Shadows sliding along the hallway. The disappointment. The fear. All gone.

One more toke before I passed it on. No, two. This stuff was great. All the bone in my spine relaxed, and I became one with the couch. The whole school floated away. Only one roadblock stood between me and complete and total bliss. Mama waiting at home. She'd want me to start dinner while she helped Spencer with his homework.

Someone handed me the bottle of wine. I took a big swallow. Mama and Spencer and Grandma were all right there in front of me, waiting, waiting, and Mama was pissed. As usual.

"Fuck all y'all," I whispered. I wasn't leaving until I had sucked the last of the marrow out of the day, and that was exactly what I did.

Chapter Eleven
Hey, Hey, We're the Monkeys, 1974

Mama borrowed the money we needed to bury Grandma. Some days she cried about everything she hadn't been able to do for her. Some days she cried because she no longer had a mother. Some days she sat at the kitchen table all day and wouldn't go to work. One day she cried about all the stories her mother told that she'd never hear again, like the one about the day she was born. But me and Spencer knew it, so we sat with her at the kitchen table while she nursed a cup of coffee.

"You were born at home in the middle of the night," I started.

"You came early," said Spencer.

"Poppy didn't want to leave, but he had to get the doctor."

"That's right," said Spencer.

The ice box rumbled in agreement.

"I was blue when I was born," Mama said.

"Grandma had to breathe the breath of life into your little lungs." Spencer pitched in.

"She was scared." I added.

"But she saved me though." Mama took a sip of her coffee.

"The doctor finally got there, and he took over, but Grandma had already done most of the work." I heard this straight from the authority on the subject.

Spencer nodded. "She got mad at him because he charged her one of her best heifers in payment."

"She didn't want to pay." Mama told us.

"But Poppy said y'all had to."

We had come to my favorite part. "Grandma said she'd always remember the tinkling sound the heifer's bell made when the doctor led it off down the road. You were crying, and she said, 'Hush, my sweet, do you hear the bell?'"

"And you stopped crying to listen even though you was only a hour old."

"She named you Pixie 'cause you was so small," said Spencer, capping off the story.

A fence of iron spears surrounded the cemetery, and the squeaking gate hung from one hinge like something from a gothic horror romance. A row of lichen pine lived between the graves and freeway, blocking the noise of the whizzing cars. The trees were tall, and when the wind blew through them, they creaked like an old wooden pirate ship. Grandma would have liked those trees.

What bugged me most about her passing was that we didn't have the cash to send her to the country to rest beside Poppy. She was buried here at Edgewood by the freeway where she didn't know a soul. Who among the stranger dead would listen to her stories? I swore that one day I'd raise enough money to take her back home.

Meanwhile, I stopped by all the time, visited her grave and got high. I talked to her more now than I did when she was at the Rainbow's Inn. She had stopped speaking when she was a patient there, but now sometimes I thought I heard her voice. Mama told everyone that Grandma was better off because she'd gone to heaven and didn't have to suffer anymore. I couldn't imagine my grandma being happy spending eternity on a white cloud. If she were in heaven, it must be more like a turnip patch.

One mushy spring day when only the dogwoods had enough faith to bud, I sat in the warm sun on a cold stone crypt, so ancient its address had worn off. The family must have been fancy and rich for a young angel stood guard. At first, she scared me. Mold grew around her eyes and in the creases of her mouth, making dark shadows. One day, when I got tired of feeling afraid, I brought a brush and scrubbed her face.

"Thank you," she said.

"You are welcome," I answered.

We'd been good friends ever since. Her name was Jane, and she was just a little bird of a thing. The index finger on her right hand was broken at the knuckle, and the nub pointed toward heaven. She told me how tiring it was to stare at the same old rocks day in, day out. The monotony gave her an ache in the wings. Jane thought a park with a fountain and children playing underfoot would have been right for her. If I had any sympathy to spare, I would have given it, but right now I was dry. She seemed to understand.

I sneezed. A bad cold had hung on for weeks, making me miserable.

I heard a tap tap tapping outside the gate, and Spoon came down the street in her trademark cosmic cowgirl boots. The gloom in my heart turned over a little. Then I saw her on the worn path between the graves. She still wore her illegal bell-bottoms, so school must have just let out. She had shaved off her bushy black eyebrows and drawn them back in a McDonald's arch. No matter what she was thinking, she always looked a little bit surprised. Daddy Spoon had made her pay for playing with her face like that, although it took him two weeks to notice the change. It was sweet that she had come looking for me.

She sat down.

"You got any more of that?" she asked.

I handed her the joint, and we sat in companionable silence for awhile. We were known regulars now at the House in the Alley, stopping for a little while every day after school. Sometimes we ran little shoplifting errands for the hippies, and they gave us our stash. We had become desperate dope fiends and had to have it all the time. So far, we hadn't gone to the back room with anyone at the House in the Alley. The girls who did that tripped down the hallway with silly giggles on their faces and came out looking like roadkill.

Mama and Spencer were always at work, so I didn't have any problem with them. Spoon told her mama that she was visiting Number Two. We usually did stop by, so it wasn't a lie. Sometimes we had a joint for good old Number Two. We had to smoke it and cover up the smell before Junior got home. As a redneck, he didn't approve.

"I came to ask you a favor," Spoon said from beside me on the crypt.

"What's that?"

"Dude asked me to go riding around with him Saturday night."

The news made me sneeze again. I wiped my worried nose, then stuffed the handkerchief back in my pocket.

"What took him so long," I asked. "Y'all been eyeballing each other for months."

"He had this thing going with Dippity-Do."

"And now he don't? You must be flattered."

"Martha, please. Don't fuss at me. I need your help." Spoon carefully rubbed out the roach on the side of the crypt. She took a pack of Kool's from her purse and put the roach in the cellophane.

Behind me, Jane the angel put both hands on her hips. She scowled on my behalf. Like I said, Jane and I had got to know each other. My story was the most interesting one she'd heard this century.

"How do I figure in this romance?" I asked.

"It ain't a romance," she said, "we're just going riding around."

Behind me, Jane shook her head.

"Number Two said she'd cover for me with Daddy but only if you go with us."

Jane rolled her eyes.

I could see exactly how this was going to play out. First, the cruise in Dude's stupid loud Camaro. Next thing I know they'd be shacking up together. No, they'd get married. That was the way the Spoon girls did things. Sheila and Dude would stand in front of the justice of the peace at city hall while businessmen hurried by swinging briefcases and making sour faces. No, the wedding would be at God's House of Whole Truth. The wheelchair boy would bear the ring. The train tunnel bum would be the flower girl, carefully leaving a trail of empty wine bottles, Four Roses. Her father, the exorcist, would escort Spoon down the aisle. The newlyweds would spend their honeymoon night at the Starlight Motel and leave the next morning itching with a bad case of crabs. Dude would cut his crowning glory, so he could cop a job at Budget Transmission. Soon I'd see my former outlaw girlfriend walking to the Piggly Wiggly with a toddler on her hip.

"There's no way I'm playing any part in this," I said, then held out my hand, "and give me that roach back."

Spoon handed me the roach. I put it in my pack of Kool's.

"What kind of chump do you take me for?" I asked her.

"I don't take you for a chump at all," she answered. "I just want to go riding around, and I want you to go, too."

"You don't want me," I said. "You want him."

Spoon pushed her hair back over one ear and stood up to leave. "I don't have time for this today," she told me.

"Then go."

"Would you at least think about it?"

"Hell, no."

"Fine," she said. She tapped tapped tapped away mumbling to herself, something about how somebody was too stubborn to do one teensy weensy favor for the only friend she had in the whole, wide world who would do anything for her, no questions asked.

Jane whispered: "Don't let Spoon get the upper hand."

"I won't," I lied.

Spoon had always had the upper hand.

"But, Jane, what am I going to do?"

Silence.

I sat there for so long my ass turned as cold as the crypt.

On Saturday night in Number Two's bedroom, Spoon made out like it wasn't a big deal, but she changed clothes seven times. She finally settled on a mini-skirt that barely covered her hiney and a tight black sweater with a purple butterfly on the front. She turned sideways in front of the mirror, sucked in her gut, and pointed to her Scarlet O'Hara waist.

"If only you didn't have to breathe, Spoon." I was leaning against the wall with my hands stuffed in my pockets.

Number Two stood in the doorway with a hairbrush in her hand and somehow looked happy and sad at the same time. Or maybe her lazy eye gave that impression since it always stared off into the distance. Number Two and Junior couldn't go riding around because their car was missing its tailpipe and two unpaid traffic tickets waiting on the kitchen table. The head of the household was in front of the television with his beer already; he had acquired the habits of a man twice his age.

Number Two said we could use her perfume. Spoon couldn't decide which one, so she wore a little of all five flavors. I didn't want any on me, and I crossed my arms. By then, Spoon leaned into the dresser mirror putting on her third coat of blue eyeshadow. She glanced at me.

"Why don't you stick out your lip, too? The picture would be complete."

"You say one more mean thing to me, and I'm going home."

"Girls, girls, girls," Number Two said, sounding as if she were forty years old. Then Number Two made me sit on the edge of the bed, brushing my hair until it crackled. "Do you want me to French braid it?"

"Sure."

Braids, French or American, were not in fashion for fourteen-year-old women, but I didn't want to hurt Number Two's feelings. Besides her hands felt good. She put her fingers deep in my hair and began to pull and twist. Just when it almost hurt, she'd let go. I couldn't remember the last time someone had fussed over me like that, but then I remembered a certain winter night lying under my grandma's wedding ring quilt, the warmth underneath, shelter from the freezing rain outside the door.

"What's the matter, Martha? You look so sad all of a sudden," said Number Two.

"Nothin'."

This time I met Spoon's eyes in the mirror. For the first time since she'd asked me to chaperone, she took a good look at my face.

"It's just a ride in the car, Martha," she said. "We'll have fun, I promise."

Number Two stared at Spoon, then at me. Back and forth. Like she was trying to figure us out.

"Thank you for going with me," Spoon added.

"You are welcome." The words tasted like quinine in my mouth.

Then Junior came down the hall, and the moment passed. He stood in the doorway and belched. "The Dude has arrived," he announced. He looked at Spoon's purple butterfly bosom, then he looked at my A cups.

"Don't worry, Martha, more than a mouthful's a waste."

Before I could say anything, Number Two put a bead on him with her strong eye while the lazy eye waltzed down the hallway.

Dude stood in the living room holding his hat in his hand, a floppy leather hippie thing. He saw Spoon and wolf whistled, reminiscent of Daddy.

Naturally, they sat up front in the bucket seats while I got wedged in back between two huge speakers. K-ROK blasted my eardrums and made my bones vibrate. All the freaks listened to that radio station, and if you didn't, you might as well kill yourself. I kept a close eye on the happy couple in the front, but they didn't go into a lip lock or anything. Nervous Spoon kept turning around to chat with me, or she stared out the window. She looked everywhere except straight at the Dude. I couldn't quite believe I was in this situation. Riding around with my girlfriend, so she could be with a guy. What kind of idiot was I? But if I didn't go, how could I keep an eye on things?

Dude fired up some Mexican Red, and I reached for it greedily and did the long suck and hold. After awhile, my blues began to disappear into the warm spring night. Then as if I had called in a special request to the radio station, the DJ played: *clowns to the left of me/jokers to the right/and here I am stuck in the middle with you.* I patted each speaker on top of the head and introduced myself.

We cruised the Dairy DeLite at three miles an hour. It was doing a great business since high flying came to town. Every pothead between the ages of twelve and twenty-five had a bad case of the munchies on this Saturday night. Thugs, thieves, and drug dealers stood on the sidewalk fingering their knives and licking double dips of chocolate chocolate. I waved, like a beauty queen, from the back seat. It was all the encouragement this one joker needed, and he rushed the car. He did the manly man handshake with Dude, but then he stuck his head in the backseat and tried to flirt with me.

"You're barking up the wrong skirt, Mister."

The joker pulled in his head like a turtle. Dude floored it, tires spun, and we split.

We stopped by the House in the Alley. It was dead for a Saturday night, but Vietnam was there as usual. He made us highballs of amaretto and Pepsi, the perfect host. Vietnam wasn't intimidating at all, once you got to know him.

Cruising by the river, over to the high school, every place our kind hung out. Sometimes huffers, who soaked rags in paint thinner and breathed the fumes, would step out of the shadows. We recognized skinny Georgia, the first girl in the sixth grade to wear red lipstick. I always thought she'd be somebody, but look at her now staggering down the street with a paper sack full of brain damage. When we were over by the bowling alley, the Camaro cut out. Carburetor, Dude said, and pulled a tire tool from under his seat. Spoon held the flashlight while he went under the hood. I watched the light play on his dirty rice face.

Then Dude had an idea of where to go, so we all got back in. He pointed the Camaro toward the nice part of town, and we began to climb the hill. We slowed in front of a stylish ranch house. Dude pointed at it with his chin.

"Three-speed bike," he said. He turned right at the corner, ran a four way stop, then left down an alley. When we were behind a huge stucco house with three dogs barking, Dude nodded toward it.

"Lawn mower," he said proudly. "Almost got caught there. Those dogs are vicious."

Spoon glanced back at me. It was my turn to raise eyebrows. She shrugged as if to say, well, what could you expect? Everybody we knew practiced the five finger discount.

Then we slowed down in front of a two-story house with white columns like a miniature plantation. Its owners probably had a portrait of their great-grandpappy in his Confederate war uniform hanging in the foyer. I had heard about places like this but never been inside one.

Dude pulled in the driveway.

I killed the joint in the backseat ashtray and snapped down the little lid that covered it.

Spoon gave Dude her question mark look.

"Did you take something from here?" she asked.

"N-o-o," said Dude, grinning.

"Well, is there something here you want?"

He shook his head vigorously, still grinning.

"Hey, this suspense is killing me." That was my voice from the backseat.

The porch light came on.

Spoon watched the front door. Then she put her hand delicately on Dude's arm. "Don't you think we'd better go?"

The gesture and her tone of voice was so much like something my mama would have done to manage Daddy that it made my chest hurt. Quickly, I collected the thought of Daddy and Mama and put it in the box where I kept all my thoughts of them. I nailed one more nail in the lid.

A man opened the door and walked out on the porch.

Oh, shit.

The man stopped on the edge of the porch and looked in our direction.

"Y'all coming in?" he called.

"Who is that?" asked Spoon.

"It's my pop." Dude was so happy with his trick. "My mom and pop live here. C'mon, they'll be happy to see us." He opened the door, hopped out, and made it all the way up to the porch before he noticed that we were still sitting there.

Dude had money; he was one of them! And we were invited in!

"This is horrible," groaned Spoon.

"This is perfect," said I.

Spoon was right. Something disastrous was about to happen. I knew it. They'd offer us hot tea in two hundred year old china cups that the ancestors had brought over from Scotland. Sugar and cream and a silver spoon for stirring. Spoon would be so nervous, she'd drop everything. I saw the thin cup shattering on an antique rug, dry clean only. I saw Mama Dude's upper lip curling in contempt. She'd escort us to the door. Proud Spoon would dump the Dude in order to save face. Who would have ever dreamed that his parents were rich? Thank you, Jesus. I was going to have Spoon back by the end of this evening.

"Bet you wish you hadn't put on seventeen coats of eye shadow, ain't that right, Spoon?"

She turned around and grabbed my leg.

"Bet you wish you'd hadn't worn that mini-skirt, huh, Spoon?"

"Martha," she cried, "I'm stoned. I can't meet his parents."

"I'm sure they're lovely people." I started pushing the back of the seat so I could get out.

Dude came back down the driveway, so she whispered: "I haven't spent any time in other people's houses. I don't know how they do things."

"Just don't hawk snot on the carpet, Sugarfoot." I am a wicked person, I thought, and it makes me happy. "And kindly let go of my leg. You're cuttin' off my circulation."

Spoon had time for one more look of misery before Dude pulled her from the Camaro.

"Hey, Spoon," I said as we were walking across the yard, "bet you wish you hadn't sprayed on all that perfume. But don't worry, I hear lots of people wear five kinds all at one time. Too bad none of them live here." I cackled like a mad wet hen.

I shook hands with Pop.

Spoon shook hands with Pop.

He turned out to be another old bald guy with big ears. Mom had to go put her shoes on, he explained. Of course, no bare feet in front of company. Their living room was long and narrow with two divans facing each other. Over one hung an oil painting of President John F. Kennedy and over the other was Jesus praying in the Garden of Gethsemane. At one end of the room, Pop had the kind of leather recliner my daddy had only dreamed about and a color television standing at attention right in front of it. A delicate crystal candy dish poised on the coffee table. Then came the kisser: the rug was the color of creamy magnolia blossoms. I had never seen a rug that color before. Far out.

Then Mom walked in. I expected someone tall and Episcopal, but she was short and frumpy. Red hair up in an old fashioned bun. She was nice to Spoon and me and asked us to sit down. She did not act mean or stuck-up. If the parents turned out to be regular, this whole thing could turn on me.

"Would y'all like a Coke?" she asked.

"Sure!" I said.

"No, thank you, ma'm," said Spoon. She perched on the edge of one of the divans with her knees pressing together, fighting with the mini-skirt and struggling to keep the possum from falling out of the tree. I sat across from her because I didn't want to miss one look of agony that crossed her traitor face.

Dude flopped down in a chair. He and Pop talked about carburetors and a mysterious thing called STP. Turned out it was something you poured in the gas tank, not something that needed treatment at the V.D. clinic.

Mom left the room. A few minutes later, she walked back in carrying a tray filled with Cokes and glasses of ice and napkins, like someone from the Late Late Show. Mom sat down, poured us drinks, wrapped the napkin around her glass. Spoon did the same thing. I tucked my napkin under my chin, sprawled my legs out in front of me, leaned back on my shoulder blades, swigged Coke straight from the bottle. I arranged my darling French braids so they stuck out in two straight lines.

Spoon flashed me a desperate telegram with her eyes.

I thought about belching.

Mom asked the usual questions: what school, which grade, favorite subject. Spoon gave back one-word answers and couldn't quite look her in the eyes. The miniskirt crept up Spoon's thigh like an unwelcome hand. The more she tugged, the shorter it got.

During a lull in the conversation, Pop looked over at Spoon and me. A big grin split his face.

"Shall we do it for them, Son?" he asked then.

"Oh, you boys," said Mom.

"Do what?" Spoon asked.

"It's just a game Pop and I play. Been doing it since I was little," said Dude.

Spoon took a polite sip of her Coke, then set the glass down on the coffee table. The lady of the house slipped a coaster under it. Spoon swallowed hard.

"Go ahead," I said, "I'd like to see your game." Maybe it required a football or something.

Dude flung his hair over one shoulder and got down in the floor on his haunches. So did Pop, with creaking knees. They began to circle each other.

I sat up straight.

Spoon couldn't have sat up any straighter.

We both turned and looked at Mom.

"It's the monkey show," she mouthed.

We nodded as if we knew what she was talking about.

"Oooh-ooh, eeeee-eeee, ahhhh-ahhh!" Dude scratched his armpits.

"Oooh-ooh, eeeee-eeee, ahhhh-ahhh!" his father answered, baring his teeth in a monkey challenge.

I'd dreamed for years about what happened in the brick houses on the hill, but I had never imagined they were mental.

The boys sprang into action. There seemed to be a dispute over some pretend bananas. Dude monkey hid them under the chair cushion. Pop monkey tried to find them. Dude monkey fought him off with one hand. Frequently, they turned to see if we were enjoying the performance. Dude and Pop were proud of the monkey show.

I turned to Spoon. She had her face set on the smile channel. One lonely bead of sweat formed at her temple and ran, like a teardrop, down her cheek. This was way better than dropping a cup and staining a rug. I couldn't have invented this. Soon Spoon and I would go home and tell Number Two and Junior about the Monkey Show. We'd laugh so hard our ribs might crack. We'd have to get down in the floor and act out a little bit. Number Two would beg us to stop before she peed her pants. Then Spoon and me would laugh one more time and go sit on the porch together. If no one was watching, we might hold hands. We might kiss. She would never look at Dude with those moony eyes again.

Meanwhile, the Monkey Show went on, but it was more interesting to watch her. Pop monkey chased Dude monkey across the living room floor. Spoon's eyes went west. The monkeys made a u-turn before crashing into the wall. Spoon's eyes followed them east. Dude monkey tried to scale the wall. Spoon's eyes climbed north. Ooops, Dude monkey crashed to the floor. Spoon's eyes fell south. Then Pop monkey got an arm around Dude monkey, and they rolled around in the floor like they was stuck together.

The oooh-oohs, eeee-eees, ahhh-ahhs rose to a high pitch then fell away. The Dude monkey allowed himself to be pinned, and the Pop monkey was King of the Swingers once again. He stood up and took a bow; the monkeys embraced. Mom applauded.

"Bravo!" I shouted, jumping to my feet. "Bravo!"

"Bravo," Spoon added. She let go of her skirt so she could clap, and the hem snapped up like a window shade.

On the ride home, Dude whistled happily.

"That was some Monkey Show," Spoon was finally able to croak.

She was still weak from the horror. Poor kid. We were going to have such a wonderful time laughing about this. Good-bye, Dude.

At the curb in front of Number Two's, I said *adios* and slipped out of the back seat. Spoon would tell him tonight that she just wanted to be friends. I waited on the front step under the porch light, so she could humiliate him in private.

Junior opened the door.

"You're not going to believe what happened!" I crowed.

"It must have been good, whatever it was." He nodded toward the car.

I turned back to see what he meant and caught sight of Spoon receiving her first man/woman kiss from the moron son of the monkey king.

Chapter Twelve

The Debutante, 1974

It was as if I lived underwater, and everything was gray and dead. Mouths opened and closed in slow motion and muffled sounds came out. People floated in and out of my vision. I was sitting in class at Jeff Davis, and the last bell must have just rung because everyone was swimming out the door. This time I remembered to follow them. Yesterday I hadn't and received a queer look from the teacher.

My dive to this underwater world started right after the night of Spoon's big smooch. On that Monday, Dude had shrieked to a stop in front of the school in his Camaro. *Honky Tonk Woman* by Big Lips and the Boys blared on the stereo. Dude wore a tank top and somewhere he had gotten muscles, even though I'd never seen him lift anything heavier than a joint. His mane of hair was glorious, and he looked like a man who could get backstage passes to anything. It didn't matter about the bad skin and the big ears. All of the kids stopped to watch, even Diane Bickerstaff Cluck and her flock of chickens. Dude hopped out of the car, ran around to the passenger side, and threw open the door with a flourish like Spoon was some kind of princess. The kids grinned at the show. A sliver of respect shot from Diane's eyes.

The featherheads would have something to cackle about for awhile.

I wished every one of them dead.

Spoon turned and asked if I wanted a ride, too, even though I had spent a great deal of time laughing at Dude and saying horrible things about him.

"If you get in with that idiot," I had told her, "I'll never speak to you again."

"Don't be like that, Martha, please." She stood to one side, so I could hop in the back seat.

"I will never speak to you again."

"Don't let your mouth write a check that your butt can't cash," she informed me.

"That is seriously profound, Spoon."

"Just get in the car."

I scratched my armpits. "Oooh-oooh. Eee-eee. Ahh-ahh."

She slung her hair back and hopped into the car. They roared off down the street, and all the color in my world went with them. They left me standing on the sidewalk, just like that. I had let my mouth write a check my butt couldn't cash. Then I remembered where I was, and who watched, and I turned and walked off in the other direction as if I had suddenly remembered an important appointment.

Now it was the last day of school. I emptied out my locker. The papers and books and pencils and my failing report card and all that other crap felt too heavy to carry home, so I dumped all of it in a trash can by the front door. Outside the crowd caught me up and pushed me across the brick courtyard. All alone in a sea of bodies. The band marched by in dull uniforms. Their grimacing faces told me they played a Requiem for the dead. Blonde majorettes strutted like hookers and pretended innocence. Miss Junior Missy was handing out red balloons. She came at me, and I flinched and turned away.

A fat kid was getting his ass kicked in the corner. It was the usual rah rah rah.

The crowd spit me out at the edge of the courtyard. A few more steps and I could put the whole lousy school year behind me. Only one more obstacle. Fair Shelby standing by the flagpole, maybe waiting for me. Shelby had done all right for himself in spite of his handicaps, hooking up with a gang of book readers. After a few weeks, he didn't want to go with me and Spoon to the House in the Alley anymore, not even for a Dude handshake. He didn't want to become a stoner. I shrugged. Better to be a stoned somebody, than a nothing nobody. Shelby moved alone. I always saw his slumped shoulders just up ahead of me. Then one day he walked out of the library with two other kids all carrying big stacks of books under their arms. They laughed at a private joke, and it was a real laugh with no sharp edges. I wanted to run up to Shelby and punch him in the arm and find out what it was all about, but then Spoon appeared, shook her head "no" when she saw what I was thinking. Spoon said they were losers. The smiling trio moved on, and my eyes followed them with longing until they were out of sight.

Today I ducked through the line of school buses to avoid Shelby. I did not want to see him standing on the sidewalk with his mouth opening and closing, like a fish drowning in air.

I drifted down the sidewalk and finally I could return to the question of the day, the week, the year. What was I going to do about Spoon? I remembered fifth grade and gave a laugh so brittle and cutting, the sound waves sliced a crow from a telephone wire. Then I thought Atomic Fire Balls would be the way to her heart. What a young dope. I hadn't spoken to Spoon since the day she rode off with Dude. At school I saw her only in the distance. She disappeared like a mirage when I got close. Of course, I walked by Number Two's house, but Dude's Camaro was always parked out front. I walked by her family's house, but I couldn't figure out when to knock on the door. I could say I was in the neighborhood and thought I'd drop by which was reasonable since we lived in the same neighborhood. I could show up as soon as she got home from Number Two's, but that would look like I had been waiting. I could go later after the supper hour. I could pretend Mama wanted to borrow something. I decided to stop by one day at thirteen minutes after six. No one had ever planned anything for that time of the day in the history of mankind, and it would look casual as if I really had been walking by her house at that moment. It would look all right. Not like I was a beggar.

But at the last second, I felt too afraid to go up and knock on the door. What if she wouldn't speak to me? I couldn't bear it if she turned her face away. All I had were questions and no answers. No one to ask.

All the furniture still outside, now broken. Moldy and skanky looking, the glamour gone. The Piggly Wiggly dumpster and the House garbage cans were having a contest to see who smelled the worse. I didn't care. Today no one was sitting out. Odd. Maybe Vietnam was having one of his attacks of paranoia, and everyone was foxholed inside. Next to the crushed VW bug, an old-timey pickup truck I had never seen before, idled on the asphalt, its keys in the ignition. For one mad moment, I thought about jumping in and escaping. Driving until I crashed. With my luck, though, I'd end up maimed, and Mama and Spencer would drag me to Whole Truth strapped in my wheelchair with no arms to reach for the suicide gun.

I knocked on the door at the House in the Alley.

No answer.

I knocked again.

Someone or something moved around inside.

What were they doing in there?

Leaning my face against the door, I waited for them to come and let me the hell in. The wood door felt cool against my cheek. I had to squint my eyes to keep from crying. These tears happened to me every time I slowed down for a second.

I had put her on the handlebars of my bike, and I did most of the pedaling. I made up games for us to play. I helped her learn how to dream after her daddy had prayed the dreams right out of her. I gave up Shelby and his gang of bookreaders for her because she said they were losers. I told her that we would have us a place to live at the beach, and she'd never have to hide when she wanted to dance. She could dance in her underpants all night long if she wanted to. Surely, I hadn't been as stupid as my own daddy, buying the wrong candy for fifteen years.

I was sick of waiting. "Open up right now!" I banged on the door.

Still no answer.

"Please, it's me, Martha." My voice trailed away. "Please."

Still no answer.

Mighty Martha, the great chicken-killer. What a joke that was. I wished the rooster had clawed out my eyes. I wished the rooster had sliced away this wanting heart of mine, so I could have just turned out regular. I thought about the Number Two in her cocoon home. Her skinny husband who slept with his arms around her so she never had to be lonely in the night. And when he wasn't there, she had four sisters and a television. She was master of her own house. Now wasn't that something?

I was so confused. My thoughts changed quicker than I could follow them, all going in different directions. Every path I took led to a dead end. Was Spoon lost to me forever? I was no closer to figuring it out than I was this morning or yesterday or last week. The tears threatened to squeeze out, and I held them back with my fists.

"I want my grandma!"

Did I just say that out loud?

Whoever was at the door chuckled.

"Ain't no grandmas here."

"What's going on?" I wiped my face and pretended everything was righteous and cool. "Where is everyone?"

"Martha," the voice said, "come back in a little while. We'll have something special." The door closed in my face.

It was a long walk home.

I heard Spencer before I saw him.

"Here she comes!" he yelled from the street corner and sprinted toward the house. He ran up the steps, and Mama stood at attention on the porch. Usually she was still at work, and he was with her or at the neighbor's. They watched me walk toward them, both trying to hide little secret smiles. Mama in a blue housedress with her hair shellacked in place. Spencer, crew cut, big front teeth, his shirt tail flopping over his jeans. What were these two demons up to? I stopped at the bottom of the steps.

"Let me guess," I said, "The Rapture is tonight and y'all got first class tickets."

My rude remark had no effect on them.

The front door opened, and Spoon stepped out of the house. She stood beside Mama and Spencer on the porch, with her hands stuck in her back pockets and a big grin on her face. Eyebrows arched in surprise. Cleopatra eyeliner. Platform shoes. Blue jeans and a short top that left her belly shining. As lush as a Luau girl.

As lush as a Luau girl?

"Hi," I said in a squeaky little voice.

"Hi," she answered.

"Sheila has a present for you," said Mama.

"Come see what it is," added Spencer.

Spoon at my house--and a present, too?

"You look snakebit," said Mama.

I wobbled up the stairs on loose knees, suddenly drunk on a voodoo cocktail of love and hope and fear. I felt like the condemned prisoner in the eleventh hour, and Spoon's presence was the delay of execution phone call from the Governor.

They pushed me through the front door before I had time to figure anything out.

A mannequin stood in the middle of the living room floor. She was bald, with her face painted on. But that was not the important thing. She was wearing a dress, a lovely old dress, turned yellow with time, the skirt covered in seed pearls, a shawl made of lace. It was like something a rich girl would wear, from the olden days. I stared, slowly walking around it in a circle. Mama and Spencer and Spoon crowded around.

"Wow," I whispered in awe.

"It's a debutante dress," said Spoon.

"An antique debutante dress," added Mama.

"It's really old," said Spencer.

"You should have seen me carrying the mannequin down the street!" Spoon laughed and slapped her knee.

The living room windows were open and the May sun caught the dress in a good light. It dazzled the eye.

"But where did you get it?" I was still walking in circles, making myself dizzy.

"I found it at the Goodwill. They had it hanging on the wall." Spoon looked at me with such pride and satisfaction. "I just got it out of layaway this morning."

"I left work early today so I could unlock the door and straighten up a little," said Mama.

"I helped," said Spencer.

I stared in astonishment.

"How did you get the money?" I asked Spoon.

"I did everything except turn tricks." She laughed again, sounding like a grown woman.

Mama blushed. Spencer wrinkled his brow.

This was both wonderful and strange. Suddenly, the people in my family were acting like regular human beings. And something had set Spoon free. Here she was wearing sinner clothes and cracking nasty jokes in front of my refried mama. I wanted to say, exactly what has happened to you Spoon, but I was afraid to jinx this moment.

Then a breeze began blowing through the windows.

"The dress is dancing!" said Spoon.

I watched with delight. A gentle wind touched a ribbon here, the skirt of pearls, the net of lace. Then the wind touched me, and I heard a waltz, and I saw the antique debutante who wore the dress so long ago in the ballroom, and the mama and the daddy who were so proud of their fine daughter, and the naughty little brother who peeked from upstairs. The wind swirled again, and the antique debutante and her friends rose up on ballerina toes, and they didn't wait for a beau to ask them to dance. They waltzed alone and together, and grace fell down like confetti.

And I knew that nowhere in the world, not even in New York City, had there ever been as anything as lovely as this. I looked at Spoon, and there was a happiness in her face I had never seen before. I put my arms around her and laid my head on her shoulder.

"I've missed you so much," I said.

"Me, too."

All the tears I'd held back started pouring out of my eyeballs. Soon we were both blowing snot bubbles and blubbering.

"I thought I'd lost you," I cried.

"No, never." Spoon stroked my hair.

I could see Mama and Spencer over her shoulder. They were smiling with shiny eyes. Everything was going to be fine.

"You didn't have to bring me a present to make up with me," I said, "but I'm glad you did. The dress is beautiful."

Nobody said anything.

Spencer turned his face away. Mama's smile held on for two more seconds, then slid off her face. I looked into her eyes and wondered why on a grand occasion such as this, what reason did she have to suddenly look so sad? I am slow, though, and didn't understand that something had just gone terribly wrong until Mama and Spencer ran out of the room like rats.

Spoon took one little step back.

"It's my good-bye present to you," she said. "Dude's father got us jobs in Mississippi. We're leaving tomorrow."

Moving slowly, she raised her hand, so I could see the ring on her finger.

Chapter Thirteen
Holding On, 1974

At the House in the Alley, I slouched on the stinky sofa half-drunk. I was there the night before half-drunk, too. And the night before that. Or maybe it had been the afternoon. Mama had even sent Spencer looking for me one day and threatened to come herself next time. Ha, ha, fat chance.

Vietnam lay across from me in a chair telling dark stories and waving his hands in the air. Nobody listened. All the freaks were putting their heads on crooked in preparation for the big rock concert across the river. They had a bonfire going under the cold night sky, and some were dancing. I watched the ashes drifting toward heaven. My feet were bare. Where had I lost my shoes?

Vietnam leaned over the coffee table and started fixing a medicinal dose of painkiller for his bum leg. His hands hovered over a spoon, a white packet, a syringe. He had f-u-c-k tattooed on the fingers of his right hand and d-u-c-k tattooed on his left. That really worried me. The saying was fuck-a-duck, not fuck-duck. Where was the missing "a"? Tattooed somewhere else on his body? What good did that do? His hands looked dumb. How was he ever going to get a wife?

Vietnam wrapped a bandana around his arm and did it right there. His tired blue eyes fluttered in his head, and his face turned to raw cookie dough. I felt embarrassed, like I had witnessed a private moment, and I shouldn't be watching. I couldn't turn away.

Vietnam had never been a soldier; it was all a big show he put on. He had wrecked his leg in a bicycle accident when he was seventeen and drunk. Swerved in front of a car and got hit. I asked him why he pretended, and he said, "Just want to be somebody, I guess." I understood everything there was to know about putting on shows, so I didn't mind all his lies. Then the next time I saw him, he was back to jabbering about hooches and Vietnamese whores, and it was like the whole conversation never took place.

"Vietnam." I leaned toward him and wiggled his knee, the good knee. "Give me some of that."

All the folks flowed by, calling their good-byes, and piling into the van. He didn't get up, not having the six bucks for a concert ticket either. But then he held out a little tray and a dollar bill, white powder in a line. He showed me how to vacuum it up my nose. We would get high, he said, and forget all about our troubles for awhile. I snorted and tasted bitter. Soon I felt a little sick, throwing up sick. But it passed. Another swallow of wine made the taste go away.

Vietnam sat beside me. I never paid much attention to him before. He was always there, like a store brand. Tonight he was really being nice, and I appreciated that. He put his arm around me, smelling like whiskey and wood smoke and a little like dirty socks and the thought of that made me bite back a laugh, a laugh that would have been hysterical and hideous. If he'd heard me laugh that way, even a medicinal dose of painkiller wouldn't have stopped him from giving me a vicious Vietnam karate chop.

My head drooped. Vietnam's arm around me was warm. He hummed a little tune under his breath and put his hand on my knee. I hoped it was the duck hand and not the other one. He kissed me. Then he stuck his wet tongue in my ear. Words moved slowly across my brain: a grown man just stuck his tongue in my ear … wait until I tell Spoon about this. Then I remembered.

Vietnam stopped.

"Don't cry," he whispered.

"I ain't crying." I rubbed my face on my sleeve.

"You been crying for days," he said. "Ever time I look at you, you're crying. I didn't know a girl could hold so much water."

I willed myself to dry up.

"Do you want me to walk you home?" he asked.

I turned, surprised, and looked at him, for the first time really.

I couldn't quite imagine us lurching down the street together.

"No, I don't want to go home."

There was no one there I wanted to see.

He kissed me again, then stopped. A second later, his head fell to his chest, and he was snoring.

It hadn't been very exciting for me, either.

I drifted in and out. Sometimes I watched the fire. Sometimes I watched the stars. Sometimes I'd think about Spoon. Sometimes I'd lean over the end of the couch and throw up. Damn convenient having the furniture outside.

Later, Vietnam shot up again. He saved some for my nose. Then I got what I really wanted. He lay on his side and made a spot for me on the couch. His arm around me, his chin in my hair, he mumbled something, a woman's name. For a second, I wondered what happened to her. But I was too tired and my bed too warm and my head too heavy to think about anything much, all of the day's devastations flying upward, like ashes from the bonfire.

In my dream, I was at the ocean doing the cha-cha-cha in the warm sand. A crowd of faceless admirers surrounded me, softly clapping their appreciation. Spoon stepped up. May I have this dance, she asked, and we began to waltz. Her face was clean of make-up, and I could smell Jergen's lotion on her skin. Everyone loved us as we swept around our sand ballroom. Around and around and around.

I didn't want to wake up from this dream. Ever. I wanted to stay here and be happy after after.

But then came a noise. A noise from outside my head that wouldn't go away. A noise that didn't belong in the show. I tried to open my eyes, but they wouldn't budge. Was someone walking down the alley? I ignored it and went on dancing with Spoon. Around and around and around. Happy after after.

But the noise wouldn't leave me alone; it was like a dog licking my face.

Someone was walking down the alley. Footsteps.

"I'll be right here," she answered, gently brushing a piece of hair from my eyes.

I landed with a thud on the couch and went back inside my body, cold and alone. Vietnam was passed out on the ground over by the dead bonfire. Before I could figure that out, the footsteps came again. I shook my head, trying to clear it. A sudden awful hope sprang up that Spoon was back for real and had come looking for me. I knew then that the evening's supply of delight was over; a wrong move in any direction would bring all the agony back. I heard it again, coming from behind me. A street lamp lit up the alley where I sat, but I could not see beyond it. I peeked over the top of the couch into the darkness.

"Here chick chick chick chick."

An old woman stepped into the circle of light.

"Here chick chick chick chick."

It was my grandma.

"Here chick chick chick chick."

She didn't look dead.

She looked solid, substantial. Not like a movie ghost who could walk through walls, but like an old country woman feeding the chickens, tossing the meal from her apron. She wore her purple dress and the sensible shoes Mama had buried her in. I made fists and rubbed my eyes. Still there. It couldn't really be her.

"Hello, Missy," she said, when she saw me peeking over the couch.

"Hi, Grandma."

"Are you awake now?"

"Just about."

She walked past the fire, stepped over Vietnam, sat down next to me. I gave her a big dopey smile. She smiled back. Was it really her? Was I awake now or in another dream? I couldn't figure it out so I gave up all disbelief and decided to go wherever this vision wanted to take me. I leaned over and put my face against her sleeve, and it tickled my nose. She smelled like my grandma, like a tomato, the first one of summer that you pick when you're still young and green yourself. She put her cheek against the top of my head and stroked my hair with her rough hand.

"Grandma," I blurted out, "are you going to have to wear that stupid purple dress for an eternity?"

"I could go naked if I wanted to," she answered. We both grinned, and her false teeth glowed in the light of the street lamp. We sat there for awhile and soaked up each other's company.

I wanted to tell her I was sorry. Sorry she had gotten so sick and my pathetic daddy had run out and we couldn't take care of her anymore. I was sorry about the nursing home: the stranger hands that touched her, the plastic flowers in plastic vases, the loneliness felt. Sorry about all the times I was supposed to visit, but didn't go.

"Grandma, about the Rainbow's Inn-"

"I hardly remember it," she interrupted, "besides, it's over."

And nothing that I had smoked or drank or said or done in the past year here at the House in the Alley felt as good as two minutes of my grandma's warm hand in my hair, loving me. I would have traded the rest of my life for the peace of that moment.

Then I heard a motor running, no louder than a cat's purr. Just coming over the rise in the alley was an old-timey pick up truck. The driver cut the headlights and glided to a stop right where we sat. Two people sat in side. An old man and an old woman. She wore a mule hat, not unlike the one my grandma owned once upon a time. He had on a pair of overalls. I should have felt surprised, but after you've lost your one true love, snorted drugs, made out on a dirty sofa with a grown man, and let your dead grandmother play with your hair, just what was there to fuss about?

"Who are they?"

"They are farmers," she whispered, "from a far off county."

Vietnam must have heard the truck, too, and it woke him. He rolled over and sat up, rubbing his bum leg, like I had seen him do a hundred times. I didn't remember when he had taken the brace off. Pushing himself up, Vietnam stood on wobbly legs and peered at the old-timers in the truck. He took a few steps, holding on to a chair for balance, still staring at the old people, unsure.

His face was a study of seriousness, like old man Noah must have looked when the dove came winging with the leaf.

The farmer rolled down his window and spit tobacco juice. He stuck out his head.

"You ready this time, boy?"

Vietnam reached into the darkness like a blind man. He toddled stiff-legged like he hadn't quite mastered the thing called walking. Then he was laughing, crying, reaching all at the same time. He was Noah with the green leaf in his hand; he was saved. The old mule hat woman threw open the passenger door, and Vietnam fell into the cab.

I had never bothered to know his real name, and I was sorry it had been like that.

With much grinding of gears and wrestling of steering wheel, the old farmer slowly backed the truck around. He waved good-bye like people do in the country. Then they drove over the rise and disappeared into the hillbilly darkness.

Grandma and I sat there and held hands.

"Why did you come here tonight, Grandma?"

"Didn't you call me?"

"But I call you all the time."

"Well," she said, "there's calling and then there's *calling*."

I nodded, searching for the difference.

"Do you remember my friend Spoon?"

"Yes."

"She was my best friend. I had no other." I held on tight to Grandma's hand. "I love her, Grandma, and she's left with Dude."

Grandma nodded, reached into her apron, pulled out a little silver can of snuff, loaded her bottom lip.

My heart broke all over again. "I'm so lost, Grandma. I don't know what to do."

"I know," she said sadly. She pulled me close again. I cried on her until the front of the purple dress was wet. She held me and her arms were as real as Vietnam's had been. We stayed like that until I was able to turn off the faucet.

"What about me being so different? How am I going to get along? Who is going to want me?"

"Martha, have you ever known me to talk with sugar in my mouth?"

"No ma'am."

"You're tough, Missy; you'll make out all right."

"You know that for a fact, Grandma?"

"Yes, indeed," She gave my hand a squeeze. "I know it for a fact."

I looked into the future, a long dirt road laid out like a ribbon. I could see only a little ways before the trees closed in.

"But what do I do right now?"

"I've always been partial to fishin' myself," she answered.

So I sat there for a long time and thought about fishing. Mostly thought about how much I hated fishing. I'd rather shoot myself twice than ever go fishing again.

Grandma reloaded her bottom lip with snuff. The street lamp blinked out. Birds began to call one another, and we watched the sun come up.

"Are you sure you're awake now, Martha?"

"I'm awake." I yawned, suddenly feeling sleepy.

"What are you going to do today?"

"I'm gonna go fishin'," I lied.

Every line on her face turned up. "I have to go now," she said, "Chores." She kissed me on the lips and gave me one more long squeeze. "Don't forget what I told you." She stood up, shook the last of the chicken meal from her apron, walked away.

I lay back on the couch and watched. I sure did love that old woman. There was so much more I wanted to say, and I struggled to hold on to the sight of her.

She turned and waved.

I called out: "What's heaven like, Grandma?"

"Like my backyard." She spit once and disappeared.

It wasn't long before all the hippies came back from the rock concert. Their noise woke me. They didn't have much luck with Vietnam though. I tried to tell them his spirit had left in the night with two old timers in a pick-up truck, that he had been ecstatic about leaving. They got pissed off and screamed *idiot* at me. What an unreasonable bunch! One of their gang finally had a cosmic experience, and no one wanted to hear about it. Dippity-Do, her hair electrified, long fingers flying, ran over to Piggly Wiggly to dial the pay phone. Sirens filled the air. In all the confusion, nobody noticed when I crawled off the couch and slipped away.

Chapter Fourteen

Goin' Fishin', 1974

On the walk home, I shimmered around the edges, like a mirage seen in the distance, still a little drunk, a little high. I had a ton of dry desert stones collected in my mouth, thirsty, and my stomach queasy at the same time. I'd be puking green for the next week. The sun bounced off buildings, blinding me, the day threatening to be a serial killer. A funky smell played Taps in the air. I suspected the smell came from me this time and not the train tunnel bum sprawled in front of the liquor store. I didn't look into his gray grizzled face, afraid of the invitation there.

Another block or two and I stumbled, ran behind a bush and heaved until nothing was left. I felt better afterwards. If my hands would stop shaking.

I sat for a while, and the morning opened up around me. A car drove by slowly, someone on her way to work, and a boy on a bike, throwing newspapers, practicing his curve.

What day was this, anyhow? I should go home and find out. I would in a minute. After I rested.

I didn't climb through my bedroom window or sneak in quietly like a criminal, which is what I would have done when me and Spoon were still in business.

This wobbly morning I opened the door and walked in like a regular member of the family, past little Brother Spencer snoring on the couch, the oldest ten-year-old in the world. I walked past Sister Pixie's closed bedroom door, then turned and went back and quietly opened it. She slept in the middle of the bed now. Always before, the right side had been hers. I didn't know how she had done it, but somehow, when I wasn't looking, she had become a woman who, instead of hugging the edge of the mattress, slept in the middle with sprawled arms and legs as if she owned the whole thing. I let myself admire her hard-headedness for just a second.

"I saw your mother," I whispered. "She's doing fine. She still loves us."

Mama mumbled in her sleep and that was enough for me.

Next, I paid a visit to an old family friend, the icebox. She gave me ice, and I made a quart jar of cold, cold water, sipped it, still not trusting my stomach wouldn't go tilt-a-whirl again. I leaned against the warm icebox and stretched my arms around her strong body and felt a little like weeping. The old girl grumbled and rumbled, keeping time, keeping time.

Mama stirred in the bedroom. Soon she'd plod in here with her hair in pink rollers and put on the percolator.

In the bedroom, I pulled off my nasty jeans. How long had I been wearing them? I opened my closet door, and at the bottom was what I needed, a box of my grandma's clothes. Right underneath the lid, I found them, a clean pair of overalls. They were still long on me, but I wasn't finished growing yet. I left one strap unhitched in Grandma's honor.

Then there was one thing left to do. It was dangerous, but I was determined. I gathered up all the Pentecostal dresses in my closet--and the false skirts, too--then put a book of matches in my pocket. I dragged the stuff out to the black spot in the yard. I made a loose pile of the clothes. Didn't turn the water hose on because I didn't care if it burned down the entire neighborhood. I struck the match and lit the hem of a particularly obnoxious number, green with baskets of fruit all over it, so ugly its creator must have been a sadist. The dress caught on fire eagerly, a suicide.

I wasn't hiding my clothes in the tool shed any longer and getting dressed and undressed in secret. I wasn't rolling my skirts up and down depending on the company I was in. If I wanted to wear a short skirt, then I'd wear one. If the Pixie from Dixie didn't like it, she'd just have to kill me. Anything less, and I'd keep going.

The fire spread to another dress, and as it grew, so did my thoughts. I wasn't hanging my head anymore. Not for Diane Bickerstaff Buck and her slaves. Not for my teachers. Not for my neighborhood. Not for this town. Not for Sister Thelma and the other church heif ers. If they didn't like it, they'd have to get in line behind Mama.

Maybe I'd join Shelby and his gang of book readers. I had always been curious about them. I opened up my mental notebook and penciled in Shelby for later that same day. I could do whatever I wanted now since Spoon wasn't here to raise her fake eyebrows at me. The heat shimmered in the air, and I felt my body shimmer too, become less substantial. The thought of Spoon did that to me. I shook those thoughts out of my head.

The fire was strong, and I didn't have to worry about it dying. Maybe it would take out the whole neighborhood and make a clean sweep of things. The flood that came through a few years ago hadn't done that, but a fire would. We could all start over.

I went back in the house to see if I had forgotten anything. In the bedroom, Spoon's mannequin stood, still wearing the lovely antique debutante dress, ugly painted on her face. I decided to have mercy and leave the dress alone. Maybe someday soon, I'd wear it to the beach, have cocktails with the seagulls.

I sat down on the creaky old iron bed to think about the beach. Just for a second before I went back outside and tended the fire. What would they be doing today? Shelby had confessed that he hadn't really gone to the beach when he was a kid. Their car had broken down in Houston, and the closest he got to water was the swimming pool at the Motel Six. But I knew that somewhere in the world, there was a beach like the one in my imagination, with hula girls dancing and pirate ships sailing and wild monkeys swinging.

On a day like today, there would be a wonderful parade. Everyone would rise up spontaneously at ten o'clock, even if they were in the middle of cutting a son's hair, or making sugar cookies, or puckering up for a smooch.

"C'mon, Martha," they'd call, "we can't start without you."

We'd drop everything and put on our costumes. Homemade costumes, of course, because it wouldn't be a competition. A boy with a silver salad bowl upside down on his head, streamers streaming in imitation of a jellyfish. A girl wearing a tail made of peacock feathers she could open and close by pulling a string. An elegant lady chicken wearing a Jackie Kennedy pillbox hat, her baby chick tucked under her wing. A flock of parrots, covered in glitter and Day Glo. A black and white orca carried by six strong men and women hidden inside. A scruffy homemade lion and a zebra with splendid stripes, walking along together holding hands. The parade ending on the sand with a band called Louisiana Hot Sauce, playing music so peppery that old animals cast down their canes and danced the Charleston.

Mama opened a cabinet door in the kitchen. She'd smell smoke soon or maybe she'd come and see if I had dragged my sorry self home. Right before she walked through my bedroom door, I saw the chicken in the Jackie hat lean toward her little one. They touched beaks, sending to each other their secret signal about love.

Sherry Clements was born and raised in Arkansas. She has a Bachelor of Arts degree from The Evergreen State College in Olympia, Washington and a Master of Fine Arts degree from Goddard College located in Plainfield, Vermont. Her job history ranges from waiting tables to being an adjunct college instructor. Today she lives in Little Rock, Arkansas, with her son, John, a mutt named Gracie, a cat named Mouse, and one recycled rabbit. A beautiful day in her life would have to include a bike ride along the Arkansas River. *The Holdouts* is her first novel.

AUTHOR PHOTO BY:
CELIA BERNHEIMER

www.ingramcontent.com/pod-product-compliance
Lightning Source LLC
LaVergne TN
LVHW090940080826
845145LV00003B/829

* 9 7 8 0 9 8 2 0 6 0 9 0 2 *